Smile

The Musical

Music by
Marvin Hamlisch

Book and Lyrics by
Howard Ashman

Based upon the Screenplay by
Jerry Belson

Originally Produced on Broadway by
Lawrence Gordon, Richard M. Kagan
and Sidney L. Shlenker

A SAMUEL FRENCH ACTING EDITION

SAMUEL FRENCH

FOUNDED 1830

New York Hollywood London Toronto

SAMUELFRENCH.COM

IMPORTANT BILLING & CREDIT REQUIREMENTS

The Authors *must* receive billing as the sole authors of the Play immediately beneath the title of the Play on lines on which no other billing matter appears as follows:

"SMILE"

Music by	Book and Lyrics by
MARVIN HAMLISCH	HOWARD ASHMAN

The names of the Authors *must* be at least 75% of the size of the title of the Play and their names *must* be equal in size, type, coloring and/or boldness and shall appear in all programs, houseboards, billboards, displays, advertising, posters, circulars, throwaways, announcements and publicity for the Play excepting only ABC ads in which only the title of the Play, theatre and/or ticket prices are mentioned. Only the name of the Licensee Producer and the title may precede the Authors' names. No name except the title of the Play may be larger or more prominent in size, type, coloring and/or boldness than the Authors' names.

The following credit *must* appear immediately beneath the Authors' credit whenever and wherever they receive credit, in size of type 75% of the size of the Authors' names:

Based upon the screenplay by
JERRY BELSON

The following credits *must* be given on the main credit page of all theatre programs, on billboards, and in all advertisements (including posters) whenever the OWNERS' credits are given:

Originally produced on Broadway by
Lawrence Gordon, Richard M. Kagan
and Sidney L. Shlenker

The following acknowledgements *must* appear in a separate box or area on the production staff information page of all theatre programs:

"SMILE" was originally
Directed by Howard Ashman
with
Musical Staging by Mary Kyte

Failure to comply with these stipulations will result in withdrawal of rights and in setting new terms consistent with Samuel French, Inc. company policy.

CAST

Contestants

ROBIN GIBSON, Antelope Valley	ANNE MARIE BOBBY
DORIA HUDSON, Yuba City	JODI BENSON
SANDRA-KAY MACAFFEE, Bakersfield	VEANNE COX
MARIA GONZALES, Salinas	CHERYL-ANN ROSSI
SHAWN CHRISTIANSON, La Jolla	TIA RIEBLING
VALERIE SHERMAN, Sacramento	LAUREN GOLER
HEIDI ANDERSON, Anaheim	DEANNA D. WELLS
PATTI-LYNN BIRD, El Centro	MANA ALLEN
DEBRALEE DAVIS, Eureka	ANDREA LEIGH-SMITH
KATE GARDNER, Fresno	MIA MALM
LINDA LEE, San Francisco	VALERIE LAU-KEE
KIMBERLY LYONS, Palo Alto	JULIE TUSSEY
GINA MINELLI, San Luis Obispo	DONNA MARIE ELIO
DANA SIMPSON, Sausalito	RENEE VENEZIALE
CONNIE-SUE WHIPPLE, Visalia	CINDY OAKES
COOKIE WILSON, Carson	NIKKI RENE
... and last year's winner, JOANNE MARSHALL	MIA MALM

Adults

BRENDA DiCARLO FREELANDER	MARSHA WATERBURY
BIG BOB FREELANDER	JEFF McCARTHY
TOMMY FRENCH, the pageant choreographer	MICHAEL O'GORMAN
DALE WILSON-SHEARS, chairman of the *Young American Miss* Foundation	RICHARD WOODS
TED FARLEY, an Emcee	DICK PATTERSON
CAROL, Brenda's assistant	RUTH WILLIAMSON
TONY, a volunteer	JEFFREY WILKINS
ROBIN's MOM/JUDGE/VOLUNTEER	LAURA GARDNER
PHOTOGRAPHER/JUDGE/VOLUNTEER	K.C. WILSON

Kids

LITTLE BOB FREELANDER	TOMMY DAGGETT
FREDDY	ANDREW CASSESE

UNDERSTUDIES

For Brenda—Joyce Nolen; Big Bob—Jeffrey Wilkins; Robin—Mana Allen, Susan Dow; Doria—Donna Maris Elio, Deanna D. Wells; Ted Farley, Dale Wilson-Shears—K.C. Wilson; Maria—Donna Marie Elio, Nikki Rene; Shawn—Lauren Goler, Deanna D. Wells; Sandra-Kay—Susan Dow, Cindy Oakes; Valerie—Andrea Leigh-Smith, Mia Malm; Tommy French—Michael Bologna.

Swings—Michael Bologna, Susan Dow, Linda Hess, Woody Howard, Joyce Nolen.

ORCHESTRA

John Beal, Michael Berkowitz, Francis Bonny, Anthony Cecere, Nick Cerrato, Andy Drelles, Dennis Elliot, Eileen M. Folson, Jack Gale, Clarissa Howell, Al Hunt, Stephen Marzullo, Ronald Melrose, John J. Moses, Brian O'Flaherty, Caryl Paisner, Dean Plank, Marilyn Reynolds, Gene Scholtens, les Scott, Ron Sell, Steve Uscher, Lorraine Wolf, Ann Yarbrough.

LUNT-FONTANNE THEATRE

UNDER THE DIRECTION OF THE MESSRS. NEDERLANDER

LAWRENCE GORDON   RICHARD M. KAGAN   SIDNEY L. SHLENKER

PRESENT

SMILE

THE MUSICAL

MUSIC BY   BOOK AND LYRICS BY

MARVIN HAMLISCH   HOWARD ASHMAN

BASED UPON THE SCREENPLAY BY

JERRY BELSON

WITH

MARSHA WATERBURY   JEFF McCARTHY
ANNE MARIE BOBBY   JODI BENSON
CHERYL-ANN ROSSI TIA RIEBLING VEANNE COX LAUREN GOLER
MICHAEL O'GORMAN   RICHARD WOODS

AND

DICK PATTERSON

SCENIC DESIGN BY   COSTUME DESIGN BY   LIGHTING DESIGN BY
DOUGLAS W. SCHMIDT   WILLIAM IVEY LONG   PAUL GALLO

SOUND DESIGN BY   PRODUCTION STAGE MANAGER
OTTS MUNDERLOH   ALAN HALL

MUSICAL DIRECTOR
PAUL GEMIGNANI

ORCHESTRATIONS BY   VOCAL ARRANGEMENTS BY
SID RAMIN BILL BYERS DICK HAZARD TORRIE ZITO   BUSTER DAVIS

ASSOCIATE PRODUCERS: BARBARA LIVITZ, RONALD AND BARBARA BALSER

MUSICAL STAGING BY
MARY KYTE

DIRECTED BY
HOWARD ASHMAN

The Producers wish to express their appreciation to the Theatre Development Fund
for its support of this production.

CHARACTERS

The Grownups

BRENDA FREELANDER — A third runner-up in the nationals, eighteen years ago, now she runs her local pageant. A study in surface perfection and just-below-the-surface neurosis, Brenda is an ex-Prom queen who lost a contest once and will *never* stop trying to make up for it. Never a hair out of place. Never a public loss of poise. She aspires to the flawless, immaculate looks and demeanor of Madison Avenue mannequins and certain television newswomen. And although she can't quite do it yet, she'll get it right if it kills her. Under all that smiling fluff, Brenda DiCarlo Freelander is made of steel.

BIG BOB FREELANDER — Her husband and head judge of the pageant. The town's favorite son, he owns a local R. V. dealership, and his every free moment is devoted to some form of community service. He's the Henry Fonda type: brave, clean, reverent, and means it. A sincere and unashamed flag-waver whose flag is this pageant. He's never been one to ask questions. Not out loud anyway. By the time this week is over, he'll have to.

DALE WILSON-SHEARS — National Chairman of the Young American Miss Foundation. A large, impressive, self-satisfied corporate leader with the suspicious charm of a television evangelist. He's in the charity business. But he's in business, make no mistake.

TED FARLEY — The pageant emcee. A professional. A big old silly. His hair is too dark for his age. Is it dyed? His cheeks are too rosy. Are they rouged? Hard to tell. He ought to do game shows. Or run for president.

TOMMY FRENCH — The choreographer, flown in to stage the pageant. He's a professional too. But a completely different kind. He's cynical, tough-minded, and practical. His chain-smoking, tough-guy stance and terminal five o'clock shadow make him comically out-of-place in this apple-pie atmosphere. Why then do we get the feeling he's the only adult around here we can trust?

CAROL — Doubles as MOTHER in PROLOGUE

WOMAN #1 — ROBIN'S MOTHER, LOUISE, WOMAN JUDGE

TONY — Doubles as a PARENT in PROLOGUE and a JUDGE

MAN #1 — PHOTOGRAPHER, ED, DADDY, MUSICAL DIRECTOR, JANITOR, JUDGE

The Girls

ROBIN — Dark, sensitive, and smart. Robin is attractive without trying to be — honest, down-to-earth, and questioning by nature. She senses that she doesn't quite belong here and over the course of the evening, she comes to understand why. She'll leave having made some important choices about the kind of women she wants to become.

DORIA — Blonde, southern, and obsessed. She *needs* badly to win something . . . anything. Perhaps to make up for the things that are missing in her real life: friends, self-respect, family. To win a Pageant has become her dream, her fantasy, her Disneyland.

SANDRA-KAY — A Redhead. Pretty but not *too* pretty. Smart but not *too* smart. Talented but not *too* talented. In short, the type that usually wins.

MARIA — Mexican-American. She tries harder. She has to.

SHAWN — A bit of a Valley Girl. Spoiled, gorgeous, competitive, and prejudiced.

VALERIE — Shawn's confidant

KATE — Doubles in Act II as JOANNE MARSHALL, last year's winner.

AND NINE OTHERS: — HEIDI, COOKIE, CONNIE-SUE, DANA, GINA, PATTI-LYNN, KIMBERLY, TRUDI, and DEBRALEE. All shapes, sizes, and levels of competence. The Young American Miss Pageant *is*, after all, for teenagers, not showgirls.

The Kids

LITTLE BOB — Son of Big Bob. Eleven years old. He has all of his Dad's surface charm and none of his integrity. He's watching his folks, alright. And picking up everything underneath their perfect exteriors. All of the bad stuff.

FREDDY — Little Bob's nerdy sidekick. Doubles as BROTHER IN PROLOGUE.

AUTHOR'S NOTE

SMILE takes place one week last summer, as Santa Rosa California plays host to the Young American Miss State Pageant. The First Act ends on a Friday evening, just after the Preliminary Competitions. The Second Act takes place on Saturday night — onstage and backstage at the Finals.

Apart from a stylized Prologue that depicts contestants getting ready across the State of California, the action of *SMILE* never strays from one building on the campus of Santa Rosa Junior College. The show should be staged simply, allowing scenes to flow smoothly and cinematically from place to place within the building: the multi-purpose room (a sort of gymnasium) where rehearsals are held, the auditorium where the Pageant itself takes place, the dormitories upstairs (dubbed "No-Man's Land") where the girls sleep, the cafeteria where they eat, and various offices where Pageant Officials do their thing. Only once — late in the second act — do we leave the building. And when we do, it's a lyrical moment. It feels good just to see the sky and stars after being cooped up in the competitive, hyped-up, pressurized atmosphere of the Young American Miss Pageant.

And what *about* the Young American Miss Pageant? What *kind* of event is it? First of all, it's for teenagers. It bills itself as a "Celebration of the Youth of America," a non-profit organization that gives scholarships. It is funded by local community service groups across the country. Ironically, the Pageant does *not* consider itself a beauty contest, even though "appearance" counts plenty and the girls *are* required to appear in leotards for the aerobics exhibition.

The Pageant does an awful lot of talking about values. But its behavior is pure show-biz. And the Pageant is thriving: waving the flag and spouting platitudes about good clean apple-pie values, while simultaneously fostering hucksterism, rampant competition, and emphasis on looks above all else. If this sounds suspiciously like certain factions in the country, it's supposed to. A good production of SMILE ought to be fast, tuneful fun . . . that carries a concealed weapon.

Howard Ashman

8

FOR BILL AND ESTHER.
AND AGAIN, FOR DAVID

PROLOGUE: Across the State of California
ACT ONE: Santa Rosa Junior College, one week last summer.
ACT TWO: The same. Saturday night.

Smile

[MUSIC # 1 *OVERTURE*]

PROLOGUE

*The audience has entered the theatre to find a bare stage and a
large video screen. As houselights dim, a well-groomed, middle-aged, corporate-looking spokesman appears on the
screen. He smiles warmly, folds his hands on the desk before
him, and speaks to us:*

WILSON-SHEARS. (*Onscreen:*) Hi. I'm Dale Wilson-Shears,
President of the Young American Miss Foundation with a public
service message from our National Headquarters in Baton
Rouge, Louisiana. I'd like to urge your local group to become a
part of the Young American Miss Experience, thus joining thou-
sands of Jaycees, Elks, Lions, Bears, Kiwanians, Mystics, and
Rotarians, nationwide. What *is* a young American Miss?

[MUSIC #2: *OPENING-TYPICAL HIGH SCHOOL SENIOR*]

(*Onscreen, the video cuts to GIRLS, answering as if being
interviewed:*)

VIDEO GIRL #1. Gosh . . . Just real average, you know.
VIDEO GIRL #2. Ordinary, really.
VIDEO GIRL #3. America's future.

(*Onstage, we now discover three real GIRLS, isolated in pools of
light. Throughout the rest of the number, the video and live
action will work together. Onscreen, we will see idealized
images of the Young American Miss at work and play. Onstage, we will gradually meet our sixteen GIRLS. At first each
is isolated in a pool of light. Eventually, as the lyrics will
suggest, the GIRLS become involved in preparation for their
departure to the pageant.*)

THREE GIRLS. (*They sing.*)
SHE'S A TYPICAL HIGH SCHOOL SENIOR

SHE IS THOUGHTFUL AND BRIGHT AND CLEAN
  SANDRA-KAY.
SHE IS CARING AND KIND.
  SHAWN.
SHE READS BOOKS TO THE BLIND
  HEIDI.
SHE'S NO OLDER THAN SEVENTEEN
  SANDRA-KAY.
AND SHE USUALLY WORKS ON 'YEARBOOK'
  SHAWN.
WHILE MAINTAINING A THREE POINT O.
  ALL THREE.
SHE'S ATTRACTIVE AND SMART,
WITH AN OUTGOING HEART
AND A VISIBLE YOUTHFUL GLOW
SHE IS EAGER TO PLEASE
YES, IN SUMMARY SHE'S
THE MOST TYPICAL GIRL YOU KNOW

*(Onstage, more GIRLS enter in pools of light. Onscreen, WIL-
  SON-SHEARS resumes speaking:)*

WILSON-SHEARS. There's one in every community. A girl who
reaches for the stars, yet keeps her tennis shoes firmly planted in
the rich soil of American tradition.
  VALERIE.
SHE'S A MEMBER OF STUDENT COUNCIL
  COOKIE.
SHE'S A MEMBER OF F.T.A.
  CONNIE-SUE.
AND YA CAN'T HELP BUT FEEL
IN A MONTH OR TWO SHE'LL
GET THE LEAD IN THE SENIOR PLAY.
  VALERIE, COOKIE, CONNIE-SUE, & DANA.
JUST A TYPICAL HIGH SCHOOL SENIOR
IN THE LAND OF THE BRAVE AND FREE
  VALERIE.
AND YOU'LL KNOW HER AS SOON AS YOU'VE
  SEEN HER
  DANA.
SHE'S SORT OF ALOT LIKE ME

ALL FOUR.
JUST A TYPICAL HIGH SCHOOL SENIOR
   VALERIE.
WHO PUTS RUM IN HER COKES
   SHAWN.
AND FREQUENTLY SMOKES
   VALERIE & SHAWN.
BUT NOT IN FRONT OF HER FOLKS
   ALL SEVEN.
LIKE ME!
AND SHE'S GOIN' TO SANTA ROSA,
WHERE THEY GATHER TO PICK THE BEST
YES, SHE'S GOIN' TO SANTA ROSA
TO COMPETE AGAINST THE WHOLE DARN WEST
WHEN I GET THERE TO SANTA ROSA
GONNA GIVE 'EM A GREAT BIG GRIN
GONNA GIGGLE AND POSE
GONNA SHOW OFF M'CLOTHES
GONNA TRY AND WHO KNOWS?
I MIGHT WIN.
   WILSON-SHEARS. (*Onscreen:*) How will you find her? Well,
when you send us your entrance fee, we'll send you a modern
video-cassette entitled The Local Pageant and How to Stage It.
Your pageant will be full of entertainment and inspiration. For
nothing brings greater joy to the real Young American Miss—
than the joy of bringing joy to those around her.

(*Six* more *GIRLS enter and sing.*)

   GINA.
WELL, HER HOBBY IS HELPING OTHERS
ALWAYS READY TO SAY "I CARE"
   PATTI-LYNN.
WHEN CALAMITY STRIKES
   KIMBERLY.
WHEN KIDS FALL OFF THEIR BIKES
   GINA, KIMBERLY, & PATTI-LYNN.
YOUR AMERICAN MISS IS THERE
   TRUDI.
SHE'S WON SEVEN FOUR-H BLUE RIBBONS
   KATE.
SHE'S A HOSPITAL VOLUNTEER

GINA.
SHE FEELS BAD FOR THE POOR
    KIMBERLY.
SHE HATES NUCLEAR WAR
    PATTI-LYNN.
FURTHERMORE SHE DOES NOT DRINK BEER.
    SIX GIRLS.
SHE'S THE TYPICAL HIGH SCHOOL SENIOR
    DEBRALEE.
THE BLOND OR BRUNETTE
    KATE.
THE DRUM MAJORETTE
    KIMBERLY.
WITH THE GREAT SILHOUETTE
    ALL THIRTEEN.
RIGHT HERE!

(*The video screen flies out. The stage is full of GIRLS now.*)

    GIRLS.
AND SHE'S GOIN' TO SANTA ROSA
WHERE THEY GATHER TO GIVE THE TEST
YES, SHE'S GOIN' TO SANTA ROSA
TO COMPETE AGAINST THE WHOLE DARN WEST
YES I'M GOIN' TO SANTA ROSA
GIVIN' OUT AND I WON'T GIVE IN
WHEN THEY START KEEPIN' SCORE
GONNA GIVE 'EM SOME MORE
CAUSE THERE'S ONE THING FOR SURE
I MIGHT WIN!

(*A kind of pandemonium breaks loose. Several PARENTS have
    entered and each GIRL is involved in packing, dressing, or
    some form of preparation for departure. Music continues
    under the following snatches of dialogue:*)

TRUDI. I'm not going.
    MOTHER. Of course you're going. You're Miss Modesto. You
won the local pageant.
    TRUDI. I *was* the local pageant. Nobody else entered.
    HEIDI. Daddy, don't eat that!
    DADDY. Why not?

HEIDI. That's my talent!
BROTHER (FREDDY). Sandra-Kay!
SANDRA-KAY. I'm not packed!
BROTHER. You've been packing since May.
SHAWN. Where the hell did I put it?
TRUDI. I am not gonna wear it.
SHAWN. Now I know it was here. Did I throw it away?
GIRLS.
SHE HAS STYLE, BUT HER TASTES ARE SIMPLE
VALERIE.
WHERE THE FUCK IS MY RALPH LAUREN?
TRUDI.
MOM, IT MAKES ME LOOK FAT!
MOTHER.
BUT IT MATCHES THE HAT
TRUDI.
COULD WE NOT GO THROUGH THAT AGAIN?
DADDY.
HERE'S THE PHONE, SAY GOODBYE TO GRANDMA
HEIDI.
BYE!
MOTHER.
FIX YOUR HAIR, STAND UP STRAIGHT
TRUDI.
YES MA'AM
SANDRA-KAY.
IS MY SNOOPY DOG PACKED?
VALERIE.
SHIT! MY FINGERNAIL CRACKED!
SHAWN.
WHERE THE HELL IS MY DIAPHRAGM?

(*For a moment, there are only two GIRLS onstage: ROBIN, a brunette, and DORIA, a blonde. ROBIN's MOTHER enters to give her a corsage and a hug. DORIA faces forward and speaks to people we don't see . . . people who obviously aren't listening to her.*)

DORIA. Goodbye, y'all . . .
ROBIN'S MOTHER. So long, sweetie.
DORIA. Gotta go now . . .
ROBIN. I'll write, okay?

DORIA. Mom . . . Dad . . . (*realizing no-one hears her*)
I'm leaving.

(*The other fourteen GIRLS and some of their PARENTS come
    crashing in. It's as if we're in an airport and everybody is
    rushing to catch a plane.*)

ALL.
SHE'S A TYPICAL HIGH SCHOOL SENIOR
SHE LIKES MUSIC AND ART AND SPORTS
    TRUDI.
MOTHER, STOP MAKING SCENES!
    MOTHER.
DID YOU HAVE TO WEAR JEANS?
WHEN I BOUGHT YOU THOSE CUTE NEW SHORTS!
    ALL.
SHE'S A PERFECTLY GROOMED YOUNG LADY
    TRUDI.
MOM, I HATE THE BARRETTES!
    MOTHER.
KEEP STILL.
    HEIDI.
HOW MUCH WEIGHT DID I GAIN?
    FATHER.
THERE YA GO, THAT'S THE PLANE!
    SHAWN. (*Still searching for diaphragm*)
WHY'D I EVER GET OFF THE PILL?
    ALL.
WELL, SHE'S NERVOUS, ALRIGHT
BUT SHE'S MAKIN' HER FLIGHT
CALL YA SATURDAY NIGHT—
SATURDAY NIGHT—
SATURDAY NIGHT—
I WILL!

(*The PARENTS are gone now. THE GIRLS are on their own,
    singing and dancing:*)

    GIRLS.
AND SHE'S GOIN' TO SANTA ROSA
REPRESENTING HER TOWN WITH PRIDE
IT'S A LONG WAY TO SANTA ROSA

BUT SHE'S READY FOR THE AIRPLANE RIDE
YES, SHE'S GOIN' TO SANTA ROSA
SORTA SCARED BUT SHE STILL CAN'T WAIT
TO ARRIVE UP IN SANTA ROSA
FORTY MILES ABOVE THE GOLDEN GATE
AND SHE'S GOIN' TO SANTA ROSA
THOUGH SHE'S NEVER BEEN THERE BEFORE
AND SHE KNOWS UP IN SANTA ROSA
THEY'LL BE WATCHIN' HER AND KEEPIN' SCORE
ON A TYPICAL HIGH SCHOOL SENIOR
GOLDEN GIRL OF THE SUNSHINE STATE
   DORIA.
WAVE AND BLOW HER A KISS
YOUR AMERICAN MISS

(*A rolling staircase moves in, like the ones used to board planes.
One by one, the GIRLS find positions on it.*)

   GIRLS.
THE BLONDE OR BRUNETTE
THE MEZZO SOPRANO
WHO'S A DRUM MAJORETTE
AND PLAYS THE PIANO
SHE'S THE ONE ON THE LEFT
JUST OUT OF HER BRACES
SHE'S THE ONE WITH CLEFT
THE FRESHEST OF FACES
HAVE YOU SPOTTED HER YET
THE ONE WHO THE WINNER WILL BE?
LOOK CLOSE, SHE'S ME!

(*Flashbulbs catch the sixteen GIRLS on their staircase,
posed . . . and smiling.*)

BLACKOUT

ACT ONE

[MUSIC #2A *ORIENTATION*]

A large, open multi-purpose room in Santa Rosa Junior College. MALE VOLUNTEERS have usurped a part of the space for set construction activities, so bits and pieces of pageant scenery are strewn about. Stage center, a small podium and several numbered tables have been set up for Orientation. Stage left is a small office area. As lights come up, CAROL and FEMALE VOLUNTEERS collate papers while WORKMEN build scenery. BIG BOB FREELANDER enters with a clipboard and surveys the bustling scene. BIG BOB is an active, outgoing, All-American type. Eighteen years ago, he was President of his senior class. Now he's President of the Santa Rosa Jaycees and runs a local R.V. dealership. He's a true believer—in his community, his country, his family, his charities, his beauty pageant. He buys it all and means every word he says. Always.

BIG BOB. Say, Tony, that looks swell.

TONY (A VOLUNTEER). We're really throwin' one this year, huh Big Bob?

BIG BOB. You're not just whistlin' Dixie, kid. Sixteen girls and Brenda tells me we got Sacramento. That's a first.

CAROL. (*To another woman as she collates, this separate conversation overlapping BIG BOB and TONY's.*) What am I gonna do, Louise? Look at his prop list. Where am I gonna find thirty-two matching umbrellas, preferably pink?

BIG BOB. Say, Tony—How 'bout how that R.V. I was showin' you over the weekend, down at the lot?

TONY. She's a beauty.

CAROL. I didn't know props for a pageant would be so hard. It was easy when the Playmakers did BRIGADOON. Just alotta shortbread and bagpipes.

BIG BOB. I don't know if I mentioned it to ya, Tony, but I'm throwin' in copperfrost appliances—and I'm talkin' trash compactors—with every baby I sell this month.

TONY. No kiddin'!

BIG BOB. And I'll tell ya what else. That beauty stores fifty gallons. Count 'em. Now in times like these, ya gotta admit it's a pretty safe feelin' sleeping on top of fifty gallons of gas.

TONY. I know, but Louise says we still oughta think about it.
BIG BOB. Yessir, Tony, you do that. You think. Thinking.
That's what recreational vehicles are all about.

(*BRENDA DICARLO FREELANDER enters, tailed by a re-
porter/photographer from a local newspaper. BRENDA is
BIG BOB's wife and in every way his match for energy and
enthusiasm. She's a perfectly groomed, perfectly organized,
perfectly lovely ex-pageant participant. But while BIG BOB is
expansive and relaxed, BRENDA betrays a touch of tension
underneath her manicured "media Mom" exterior. She's
trying too hard.*)

BRENDA. Mother Hens, mother hens. These have to be col-
lated and put into three separate piles per coop. Also the name
tags and Carol, would you run on up to No-Man's Land and
make sure they've got the linens finished? Oh Bob, there you are!
Good.
BIG BOB. Be right with you, Brenda. (*to TONY*) Here's my
card. You call me anytime you make up your mind. Big Bob's
customers are also his friends.
BRENDA. Bob—this is Dave Schultz from the Santa Rosa
Clarion.
DAVE. Say, You're Big Bob Freelander's Motor Town aren't
you?
BIG BOB. That's me. "Where a Boy gets the best for the buck
that he spends . . ."
BOTH. "Because Big Bob's Customers are also his friends."
DAVE. That's one heck of an ad.
BIG BOB. We all love it at my house.
BRENDA. Call and beg Mr. Mason. We can't rehearse without a
piano. Remind him he's an Elk.
CAROL. He's not an Elk.
BRENDA. Well then remind him he's a Christian.
DAVE. And you're in charge of the pageant?
BIG BOB. Me and Brenda. She's JayCette Pageant Coordinator.
DAVE. And you two were last year's Jaycee Family of the Year?
BIG BOB. Not by ourselves. Little Bob. . . . Come over here
son. This gentleman wants to take our picture.
DAVE. That's Bob Junior?
BIG BOB. Little Bob.

DAVE. Okay, folks. Smile. (*snaps photo*) Thanks alot. This'll be out on Wednesday. (*exits*)

BRENDA. Don't forget to mention that tickets are still available — both nights.

BIG BOB. Both big nights! (*As he and BRENDA move toward the office area*) Oh, Brenda — Tommy French's agent just called. He's been detained at Lake Tahoe and won't arrive until tomorrow morning.

BRENDA. (*Opening mail*) Tomorrow morning? At what we're paying him?

BIG BOB. Expensive people are always late. That's why they're expensive.

BRENDA. Oh, Bob . . .

BIG BOB. What is it, dumplin'? What's wrong?

BRENDA. Mr. Shears. Mr. Wilson Shears. Dale Wilson Shears. The National Chairman.

BIG BOB. What about him?

BRENDA. He's coming.

BIG BOB. To our pageant?

BRENDA. Preliminary Night. With French late, half the props still missing, the set behind schedule . . .

CAROL. Brenda! They're here! They're getting off the bus!

BRENDA. He's coming. Why would he be coming? There's an opening on the National Committee. (*softly and intensely, electricity crackling*) You don't think they're considering me, do you?

[MUSIC #2B *THE CONTESTANTS*]

(*Suddenly, the babble of sixteen excited teenagers fills the air and the GIRLS come bombing in, chattering away. CAROL ushers them toward the Orientation area, then ascends the rostrum and tries to make order. It's hopeless.*)

CAROL. Alright, girls. This way. This way. Now take seats, girls. Find yourselves a place to sit. You'll need a pen, paper, and . . . Attention girls! Please! We've got to start! Now I'd like to introduce the Coordinator of our State Pageant, a former Young American Miss herself, Mrs. Brenda DiCarlo Freelander.

[MUSIC #3 *THE VERY BEST WEEK OF OUR LIVES*]

BRENDA. (*ascends the rostrum and smiles*) Hi. I hope you all were listening and picked up your pens, because you may want to take notes. The next six days will be the busiest and most wonderful of your lives. So savor each moment, girls. As anyone over thirty can tell you . . . It'll never come again.
THE VERY BEST WEEK OF YOUR LIVES
THE VERY BEST WEEK OF YOUR LIVES

UP AT SEVEN, GRAB A SHOWER,
GULP BREAKFAST DOWN IN HALF AN HOUR
'CAUSE EIGHT O'CLOCK,
YOUR FIRST REHEARSAL'LL START
CAROL'S PASSING OUT THE SONGS WE'LL USE
    THIS YEAR
PLEASE LOOK AT THE MUSIC
AND LEARN ALL THE LYRICS BY HEART
WORK TIL FIVE WHEN TIME'S UPON US
TO MEET THE JAYCEES AND KIWANIS
YOU'RE GONNA LOVE ALL OF THEM AND THEIR
    WIVES
REMEMBER THEY'RE YOUR FRIENDS AND LOCAL
    SPONSORS OF
THE VERY BEST WEEK OF YOUR LIVES

(*Orientation activities proceed throughout the rest of the number. GIRLS form lines to fill out forms, receive name tags, etc., shepherded with merciless good cheer by BRENDA and her helpers. We focus for a moment on two of the GIRLS, the blonde and brunette we remember from the opening number:*)

DORIA. Hi. I'm Doria Hudson. Yuba City.
ROBIN. Robin Gibson — Antelope Valley.
DORIA. It says here we're bunk sisters. Does that mean roommates?
ROBIN. I think so. (*Our focus returns to BRENDA.*)
BRENDA.
TUESDAY, AFTER COSTUME FITTINGS
WE HEAD DOWNTOWN FOR PHOTO SITTINGS
WE GO BY VAN — MY HUSBAND ROBERT DRIVES
HE'S MY STRONG RIGHT ARM AND ALSO YOUR
    HEAD JUDGE
THIS VERY BEST WEEK OF YOUR LIVES

BIG BOB. Now girls, we do have a few rules. Simple ones. No smoking. No drinking. And no . . . uh . . . no boys. (*GIRLS react. BRENDA teases.*)

BRENDA. I know, I know. But it's just a week. And what a week.
THE BEST SEVEN DAYS OF YOUR LIVES
MAGIC MOMENTS AND MORE THAN A FEW.
WANNA KNOW HOW I KNOW? WELL, YOU SEE,
  LONG AGO
I WAS SITTING THERE. I WAS ONE OF YOU . . .

CAROL. Girls, I have an additional announcement. Your luggage will be arriving . . . (*BOB hands her a note.*) Er . . . Some of your luggage will be arriving shortly. (*GIRLS react loudly as CAROL continues.*) There's been a mix-up at the airport and . . .

BRENDA. (*interceding*) Ladies, please . . .
DO US ALL A SPECIAL FAVOR
AND HELP CREATE BY YOUR BEHAVIOR
AN ATMOSPHERE WHERE BEAMING TEAMWORK
  THRIVES
I SEE FROM YOUR FACES WE CAN COUNT ON THAT
AND SO 'TIL YOUR LUGGAGE ARRIVES—
WEAR YOUR NAMETAG, YOUR SASH,
AND A SMILE CHEEK TO CHEEK
AND WATCH OUT FOR THE PIPES IN THE
  BATHROOMS,
THEY LEAK
STILL THEY'RE PART OF THE START OF
THE VERY BEST WEEK OF YOUR LIVES—

Have a terrific evening, girls . . .
We turn lights out at ten . . .
Get lots of sleep
You'll need it . . .

(*The girls are offstage now. BRENDA moves to the office area and sinks into a chair. CAROL follows.*)

CAROL. Brenda, it's about these props. I don't know if I can handle it.

BRENDA. Of course you can. All it takes is a drop more energy, a drop more optimism, and a drop more perseverance.

CAROL. That's so beautiful.

BRENDA. Here are a few more things I'd like you to pick up on your rounds.

CAROL. Typed. You're so organized. How do you do it?

BRENDA. I don't know. I get tired. But I just keep going. (*CAROL exits.*)

BIG BOB. You are amazing.

BRENDA. Not so amazing. I haven't even thought about dinner. Little Bob, how hungry are you?

LITTLE BOB. Oh, somewhere between Zimbabwe and Biafra.

BIG BOB. That's not funny, son.

LITTLE BOB. Sorry, Dad.

BRENDA. Bob, give him some money to run down to Jack-in-the-Box with, will you? (*BIG BOB gives LITTLE BOB some cash. LITTLE BOB exits.*) I thought I'd microwave us some lasagna at home.

BIG BOB. Hey — M'favorite. But y'know hon, that hour and a half drive doesn't make a whole lotta sense when we're due here again at sunrise. (*He massages her shoulders as he speaks. She keeps right on working. It's a sad seduction attempt on his part. Either she doesn't notice or doesn't want to.*) How about I ring the Quality Court and get The Family of the Year a couple rooms? One for Starving Offspring and one for the Happy Couple. I'll get room service to throw on a couple Chicken Kievs and a bottle of Mateus. By morning I'll see that you're a new woman.

BRENDA. Oh fudge, where are those applications?

BIG BOB. So whatdya say?

BRENDA. Hm?

BIG BOB. About the motel.

BRENDA. (*sweetly matter-of-fact*) A motel tonight? Bob, you know I'm restless in a strange bed.

BIG BOB. Aw c'mon.

BRENDA. (*as she exits*) I'll unwind while you drive and be asleep before my head hits the pillow. You'll see.

BIG BOB. (*to himself*) Yeah.

[MUSIC #3A *SCENE CHANGE* 1]

(*Lights dim on the multi-purpose room and come up in "No-Man's Land," the dormitory area where GIRLS are getting ready for bed. First, we focus on the shower-room. ROBIN, DORIA, and several other GIRLS are washing up at the sinks. MARIA is strenuously doing exercises. Nearby, she has stashed a large brown shopping bag. SHAWN is drying her hair and observing MARIA in semi-amusement.*)

SHAWN. You do this every night?
MARIA. Si. Mornings too.
SHAWN. Mexicans have to work to maintain, huh?
MARIA. We gotta work to do everything.
SHAWN. Not me. I can eat anything I want, don't knock myself out in Phys. Ed. and I just stay the same. I think it's genetic. (*beat*) Maria, I hope you don't mind but that bag over there, I looked in it . . . by accident.
MARIA. That's okay.
SHAWN. Yeah, well, it's full of avocados.
MARIA. Si.
SHAWN. Well . . . how come? Are you a juggler or something?
MARIA. (*stops exercising and turns to SHAWN with a smile that says 'I've got your number.'*) I am so glad you are my roommate. You are a very nice person. And you are very funny.

[MUSIC #3B *SCENE CHANGE* #2]

(*MARIA goes into a shower-stall and closes the door. SHAWN just stares after her, then exits. Lights shift to focus on ROBIN, who has discovered something in a cabinet under the sink:*)

ROBIN. Doria . . . there's all kinds of man's shaving stuff under the sink.
DORIA. Yeah, the track team used these dorms last month. What are you doin'?
ROBIN. Just looking at it. Believe it or not, I've never been in a bathroom a man uses before.
DORIA. Well, me neither . . . hardly.

(*Lights follow ROBIN and DORIA as they leave the bathroom and head toward their bedroom, a short distance away. During the following, ROBIN and DORIA get ready for bed.*)

ROBIN. Oh, I didn't mean that. I just meant I never had a father or brothers or anything. Back home, it's just me and my Mom.
DORIA. Divorce huh? Tell me about it. My Mom's so busy

trying to figure out who to marry next, she hardly has time to eat lunch. My brother Joe was lucky. He got a job and lit out at fifteen.

ROBIN. Well, my folks aren't divorced. My dad's not living. He died in a car wreck when I was three.

DORIA. I'm sorry, Robin.

ROBIN. Oh, it's okay. I don't even remember him.

DORIA. You know, it could help you in this contest . . . getting to be a top high school senior without a father to help you. Jesus, listen to me. Was that a horrible thing to say?

ROBIN. I don't think so. You really think stuff like having no father counts up here?

DORIA. Everything counts up here. Your talent, your personality, the judges conference. (*beat*) Is this your first?

ROBIN. Sure. In fact I didn't even enter by myself. Mrs. Owens, our class sponsor, sent in my name and then she told me. God, I never thought I'd win. (*beat*) Is it your first too?

DORIA. Heck no. I was Miss Teenage Complexion, back in Waco, Texas.

ROBIN. I don't think I've heard of that one.

DORIA. It was sponsored by this horny dermatologist. He rented a room at the Quality Court, got sixteen girls in bathing suits and had his own beauty contest.

ROBIN. You're kidding.

[MUSIC #4 *DEAR MOM* #1]

DORIA. This is my first contest since we moved to California, though. Contests are better here. More of 'em, stiffer competition, but if you win, it means something. I've been checking into it. There's Miss California Fruits, Miss Wine Country, Miss Golden Gate, Miss Marineland, Miss . . .

(*DORIA continues babbling, but lights dim on her a bit and focus instead on ROBIN, who is writing a postcard:*)

ROBIN.
DEAR MOM
I'D LIKE TO SEE THIS WHILE I'M HERE, MOM
IT'S A PICTURE OF THE HOUSE OF LUTHER BURBANK
IT'S WHERE HE'S BURIED

THOSE ARE HIS GARDENS
PRETTY HUH?

DORIA. And of course everywhere there's Miss Teenage America, Miss Universe, Miss World, Miss . . .

ROBIN.
WELL, MOM
HAVEN'T GOT ALOT TO TELL, MOM
NOTHING'S HAPPENED YET.
MY ROOM-MATE'S VERY FRIENDLY
LOVE TO PHIL AND GENE
P.S. DIDN'T LUTHER BURBANK INVENT THE
  NECTARINE?
LOVE,
ROBIN

DORIA. And then, of course, someday . . . Atlantic City.

ROBIN. You know alot about Pageants.

DORIA. It's my hobby, practically. Ask me who was Miss America — any year, any year at all.

ROBIN. 1959

DORIA. Mary Ann Mobley

ROBIN. 1965

DORIA. Vonda Van Dyke.

ROBIN. Wow.

DORIA. Ever since I saw my first one. She was standing in Disneyland.

ROBIN. Disneyland?

DORIA. I was just a kid. They had this special, you know. Live from Disneyland. And there she was . . . that year's Miss Anaheim. All dressed in white and waving. And Mickey and Donald and Goofy and everybody bowing and scraping and dancing around. I'm gonna enter Miss Disneyland too, soon as I'm old enough. God, I'm dying to see it.

ROBIN. I hope you're not disappointed.

DORIA. Whatdya mean?

ROBIN. I mean I've been there and it's kinda creepy. Mostly gift shops and people wearing costumes with very big heads.

DORIA. Oh come on, Robin. It looks fantastic. Castles and bobsleds and magic mountains . . .

ROBIN. Yeah, but they're all made of plaster and chicken wire. When I was there, I heard some birds singing, you know? And I looked up. There were speakers in the trees. I mean I guess it looks

pretty in a tacky sort of way, but it's phony as anything. Goodnight, Doria.

[MUSIC #5 *DISNEYLAND*]

DORIA. Goodnight, Rob.

*(The lights are out now. ROBIN has curled up and fallen quickly
asleep. DORIA sits on the edge of her bed, lost in thought.
She sings:)*

HOT SUNDAY NIGHT
I GUESS THE FOLKS WERE BUSY FIGHTIN'
JOE'D ALREADY LEFT HOME
ELEVEN YEARS OLD, ON MY OWN,
FEELIN' NOTHIN' BUT LONELY.
THERE'S NOTHING TO DO,
THERE'S NOTHIN' OUT THERE BUT THE TRAFFIC
DOWN ON STATE NINETY-THREE
SO I'D SIT THROUGH THE NIGHT
BY OUR OLD BLACK-AND-WHITE TV.
AND THAT'S WHERE I SAW IT—
THAT'S WHEN I HEARD IT—
CALLIN'
CALLIN'
ME

DISNEYLAND
MAGIC KINGDOM, DISNEYLAND
CLOSE MY EYES REAL TIGHT
WISHIN HARD I MIGHT, WISHIN HARD I MAY
FIND MY WAY TO DISNEYLAND
GOTTA GET TO DISNEYLAND
ON A WESTERN BREEZE, MAGIC CARPET PLEASE
CARRY ME AWAY

OH I KNOW YOU'RE GONNA SAY
THE TREES ARE PAPER MÂCHÉ
IT'S DONE WITH MIRRORS, THE MAGIC THERE
EACH LITTLE BIRD'S FULL OF SPRINGS
YOU PRESS A BUTTON, IT SINGS

RECORDED MUSIC IN THE AIR
THEY'VE HAD THE MOUNTAIN RE-FACED
IT'S ONLY PLYWOOD AND PASTE
GO ON SAY IT
I'LL TURN AROUND AND TELL YOU I DON'T CARE!
I DON'T CARE
I WILL LIVE IN

DISNEYLAND
MAKE MY HOME IN DISNEYLAND
MAYBE IT'S ALL FAKE, THAT'S A CHANCE I'LL TAKE
IT'S PERFECTLY OKAY . . .
SOMEONE GIVE ME DISNEYLAND
TAKE ME THERE TO DISNEYLAND
AND WHEN I GET TO DISNEYLAND
I'LL STAY.

[MUSIC #5A *SCENE CHANGE* #3]

(*Blackout. When lights restore, we're in the multi-purpose room, the next morning. Lights find LITTLE BOB on the phone in his parents' office area.*)

LITTLE BOB. How should I know, Freddy? They don't write down whether they're virgins. The point is, there's a place upstairs called No-Man's Land, where they all go to get naked so . . . (*BIG BOB enters office.*) No, I can't go bowling, Freddy. Bye.

BIG BOB. (*rummaging through a file cabinet*) Now I know sure as shootin' those applications were in here.

LITTLE BOB. (*handing him a manila folder*) Were you looking for these, Dad? I was just reading some of them.

BIG BOB. You were?

LITTLE BOB. Uh huh. I know I sorta put this pageant down the last couple years, but reading these applications . . . I mean I can see why you want to help these girls. They seem . . . uh . . . very worthwhile.

BIG BOB. Right on, son. These are the finest bunch of high school about-to-be-seniors in the state. (*beat*) And ya know what else? One of the very best things about growing up is one day you wake up and find yourself interested in all sorts of new things.

LITTLE BOB. Yeah.

[MUSIC #5B *SCENE CHANGE* #4]

(*Lights dim in the office and come up on the large open space
where the GIRLS have been assembled and BRENDA is
addressing them. She stands beside an enormous lobby photograph of TOMMY FRENCH, the pageant choreographer.*)

BRENDA. (*reading from his bio*) The wizard behind dozens of
popular stage shows in Las Vegas, Atlantic City, and Six Flags
Magic Mountain, Mr. Tommy Douglas French is equally at
home in film and television, having choreographed such stars as
Merv Griffin, Wink Martindale, and Phyllis George. (*TOMMY
enters, to one side, unnoticed by anyone except a JANITOR.*)
JANITOR. Sorry buddy. No men allowed in there.
TOMMY. It's okay. I'm a choreographer.
BRENDA. (*as TOMMY enters and stands watching her*) His
extensive summer stock credits include fifteen separate produc-
tions of Hello Dolly with stars ranging from Phyllis Newman to
Jean "Edith Bunker" Stapleton. In 1976, his staging of a Bicen-
tennial Salute to Broadway at . . . (*She turns and sees
TOMMY, standing in front of his photographed — and air-
brushed — image. This chain-smoking, unshaven, heavy-lidded
man bears little resemblance to his scrubbed and grinning
publicity shot.*) Ladies . . . Mr. Tommy French. Mr.
French . . . Our Girls.
TOMMY. Coffee.
BRENDA. Coffee. Carol —
TOMMY. Alright — the theme of this year's pageant
is . . . (*takes a deep drag from his cigarette*)
BRENDA. Health and fitness.
TOMMY. Have any of you girls had any dance experience?
SANDRA-KAY. Does square-dancing count?
TOMMY. Not with me, dear. Alright, let's see what we've got
here. Grab a pole and form two lines —
BRENDA. Poles! Lines! Carol — Louise! (*She leaves CAROL in
charge and exits quickly. The GIRLS grab bamboo poles from a
pile and form their lines.*)
TOMMY. (*demonstrating a slick pole-juggling maneuver*) Two
lines. Straight lines. Now it's down, kick, toss, catch. Got it? Try
it. Down, kick, toss, catch. (*The GIRLS try. A noisy disaster.*) A
showstopper.

[MUSIC #6 *SHINE*]

(MUSIC IN. BRENDA sweeps downstage, lights change, and we are momentarily transported to a Lions' Club luncheon:)

BRENDA. Yes, all of you folks down here at the Lions can be proud of your annual pageant sponsorship. And right after lunch, which I hear is delicious, you'll meet some of this year's delightful contestants. We're looking not just for physical beauty, but a girl with poise, personality, and promise. Remember, the pageant is not a meat show.

(Lights dim on BRENDA and return to the multi-purpose room, where Tommy demonstrates a dance step:)

TOMMY. Thrust with the pelvis and . . .

(Some of the GIRLS, gathered at a piano, begin to sing from sheet music. Others try their best to keep up physically as TOMMY demonstrates a dance routine. The following number, SHINE, is a fast-paced montage sequence that simultaneously follows BRENDA's day and the GIRLS' rehearsal with TOMMY FRENCH. The number he teaches them is a strenuous, aerobics-oriented dance routine. It's tough and TOMMY pushes the GIRLS hard.)

GIRLS.
I'VE LEARNED SOMETHIN' INSPIRATIONAL
I'VE GOTTA SHARE IT
IF YOU WANNA BE SENSATIONAL
THIS WORKS, I SWEAR IT
YOU GOTTA WAKE UP EVERYDAY
ROLL RIGHT OUTA BED, STRETCH, AND THEN SAY —
OKAY!
GONNA SHINE, SHINE
UP TO NOW I HAVEN'T PRESSED MYSELF
GONNA SHINE, SHINE
FACE THE WORLD AND REALLY TEST MYSELF
GONNA SHINE, SHINE
GONNA BETTER, GONNA BEST MYSELF

TOMMY.	GIRLS.
One and two and three and four	I'LL LAY IT ALL OUT ON THE LINE!

Five, six . . . Again!
GIRLS.
GONNA SHINE!

(*Lights plunge the dance rehearsal into silhouette, an Elks logo flies in, and a spotlight finds BRENDA at the Elks Club with several of her GIRLS. She immediately turns the podium over to one of them: SANDRA-KAY, a wholesome, rosy-cheeked, 'old-fashioned' girl to whom all of this comes very naturally.*)

SANDRA-KAY. (*taking the podium from BRENDA*) Hi, I'm Sandra-Kay MacAffee, Bakersfield's Young American Miss. I'm really glad to be here with all of you Elks, 'cause my Dad's been an Elk for fifteen years. It's really helped me understand that no matter how busy we may be—there's always time for community service.
GIRLS.
SHINE! SHINE! SHINE! SHINE!
SHAWN. (*replacing SANDRA-KAY at the podium*) Hi, I'm Shawn Christianson, La Jolla's Young American Miss, and I'd like to invite you all to come spend time in beautiful Southern California. We're all concerned about preserving our state's magnificent natural resources. Well, there's no better way to start—than with a visit to Marineland! (*BRENDA and the GIRLS exit. Back at the ranch, rehearsal continues:*)
GIRLS.
YOU'LL FEEL ABSOLUTELY WONDERFUL
WHEN YOU DECIDE IT
YOU'LL FEEL HEALTHY AND JANE FONDA-FUL
I KNOW, I'VE TRIED IT
I SIMPLY WAKE UP EVERYDAY
OPEN UP MY EYES, STRETCH, AND THEN SAY—
OKAY!
GONNA SHINE, SHINE
I REPEAT IT WHEN I RISE MYSELF
GONNA SHINE, SHINE
AND I FIND THAT I SURPRISE MYSELF
GONNA SHINE, SHINE
EXTROVERT AND EXERCISE MYSELF

TOMMY.	GIRLS.
One and two and three and four	I KNOW THE WORLD'S GONNA BE MINE!

Five, six . . . Again!
    GIRLS.
IF I SHINE!

(*The rehearsal goes back into silhouette. Downstage, BRENDA
re-enters with DORIA, ROBIN, and MARIA GONZALES.
A Rotary Club logo flies in behind them. DORIA is first to
speak and she does so with relish and the air of a true cheer-
leader. It's clear she has worked on this:*)

DORIA. Hi. I'm Doria Hudson, Yuba City's Young American
Miss, and I want to tell you how lucky I feel to be here in beautiful
Santa Rosa. I always thought our shopping mall back home
was really something. And then I saw yours. It's . . . a
credit . . . to the Vision of your Business Community.
    GIRLS.
SHINE! SHINE! SHINE! SHINE!
    MARIA. (*takes the podium, holding a hand-painted clay bowl,
covered with Saran Wrap*) I am Maria Gonzales . . . Salinas'
Young American Miss. And since you gentlemen have been nice
enough to feed us, I would like to feed you . . . With this homemade guacamole dip . . . it is a typical dish of my native
land—*Mexico*!
    GIRLS.
SHINE! SHINE!

(*It's ROBIN's turn. She timidly approaches the podium. DORIA
practically has to push her.*)

ROBIN. (*almost   inaudibly*)   Hi,   uh . . . I'm   Robin
Gibson . . .
    GIRLS.
SHINE!
    BRENDA. Speak up, dear.
    GIRLS.
SHINE!
    ROBIN. (*too loud now*) Robin Gibson. Antelope Valley's
Young American Miss. (*Beat. Terror. Then, miserably:*) Thanks
for having me to lunch. (*BRENDA and the GIRLS exit as the
rehearsal plows downstage and takes over the playing space. The
GIRLS who dance are improving—a little.*)

GIRLS.
GONNA GLOW, GONNA GLEAM, GONNA GLIMMER
THAT'S WHAT I MEAN WHEN I SAY GONNA SHINE
GONNA BURN, GONNA TURN UP MY DIMMER
GONNA BE THREE HUNDRED AND FIFTY WATTS
    OF DIVINE
GONNA SHINE!
    CAROL. (*in rhythm*) Ten minute break! Milk and twinkies in
the conference room.
    LOUISE. (*in rhythm*) Talent rehearsal. Room 415!

(*Lights find TRUDI doing scales on a trombone for a grimacing
    MUSICAL DIRECTOR.*)

    MUSICAL DIRECTOR. Thank you.
    TRUDI. Thank you.
    CAROL. Thank you.

(*Lights dim on them and come up on MARIA, giving rapid-fire
    instructions to a STAGE MANAGER.*)

    MARIA. It's a musical home economics demonstration, very
difficult, so timing is everything. It's all on this sheet so you can
study it. I hold up the chili rellenos, applause, applause, applause,
you hit me with the spot. I do the break, say "clever mamacita."
Laugh, laugh, laugh. I gesture. Cue tape with my backup singers.
You got it?
    CAROL. Are you ready, Maria?
    MARIA. (*The smile is back.*) Si! (*And she is swept into a group
of madly dancing GIRLS:*)
    GIRLS.
YOU SAY OH I'M SO DE-ENERGIZED
WE'VE ALL BEEN THROUGH IT
I SAY YOU CAN BE BRUCE JENNER-IZED
HERE'S HOW TO DO IT
YOU GOTTA WAKE UP EVERYDAY,
ROLL RIGHT OUTA BED, STRETCH, AND THEN SAY
OKAY!
GONNA SHINE, SHINE—
    TOMMY. Kick and bend and kick and bend.
    GIRLS.
GONNA SHINE, SHINE

TOMMY. Turn on the left foot back to the other step.
GIRLS.
GONNA SHINE, SHINE
TOMMY. Kick and bend and kick and bend and . . . No
honey, if you kick and bend at the same time you'll knock your-
self out.
GIRLS.
GONNA SHINE!
BRENDA. (*enters downstage, talking to CAROL, who takes
notes*) His name is Shears . . . Dale Wilson Shears. They're
holding a suite for him at the Ramada. See that he gets the V.I.P.
treatment! Chocolates and a bowl of fruit! A limousine should be
at the airport. Maybe a small champagne reception . . .
TOMMY. Jump! Jump! Jump!
Jump! Jump!

(*The dance routine has cleared the stage for a moment. Lights
focus on BRENDA, as she sings her thoughts:*)

BRENDA.
EIGHTEEN YEARS AGO . . .
WAS IT REALLY THAT LONG AGO?
THE PAGEANT THAT I WAS IN
. . . WHEN I DIDN'T WIN.

EIGHTEEN YEARS AGO . . .
BATON ROUGE WAS THE MOST EXCITING
PLACE I HAD EVER BEEN—
AND I DIDN'T WIN.

(*In dim light, upstage of BRENDA, GIRLS slowly begin to re-
enter in a choreographed, circling formation. Their movement is dreamlike and stylized. They carry Cheer-leader-
style Pom-Poms. As BRENDA's soliloquy builds, more and
more GIRLS carrying paper Pom-Poms begin to fill the stage
with contained, rhythmic movement.*)

I THINK BACK ON THE GIRL THAT I WAS AND I
    PITY HER
SO MANY OTHERS WERE GLOSSIER, PRETTIER
KNEW HOW TO STAND HOW TO MOVE, WHERE
    TO GO

OH BUT THEN THERE WAS BRENDA, POOR MISS
  CALIFORNIA
UPTIGHT IN THAT SPOTLIGHT AND NO—
NO, EIGHTEEN YEARS AGO IS THE PAST. THAT
  WAS THEN.
NOW THEY'RE COMING AT LAST, HERE TO JUDGE
  ME AGAIN
OKAY LET THEM COME DOWN HERE TO JUDGE
  ME 'CAUSE WHEN
THEY ARRIVE THEY WILL SEE THAT I'M NOW IN
  MY PRIME
I CAN HANDLE THE SPOTLIGHT, THE PRESSURE,
  AND I'M
FINALLY READY . . . I'M SURE THAT I'M READY
TO WIN THIS TIME!

(*Light change. The dreamlike mood of BRENDA's soliloquy is
  shattered. THE GIRLS' Pom-Pom routine busts loose. If
  they have been improving gradually throughout the
  "SHINE" sequence, now, with Pom-Poms, they're a fighting
  machine. BRENDA's melody line and the number the
  GIRLS have been rehearsing come together as the sequence
  builds to a close:*)

  GIRLS.
I'VE LEARNED SOMETHIN' INSPIRATIONAL
I'VE GOTTA SHARE IT
IF YOU WANNA BE SENSATIONAL
THIS WORKS, I SWEAR IT
YOU GOTTA WAKE UP EVERYDAY
ROLL RIGHT OUTA BED, STRETCH, AND THEN SAY—
(AND THEN SAY AND THEN SAY AND THEN SAY AND
THEN SAY AND THEN SAY AND THEN SAY:)

GONNA SHINE!
  BRENDA.
THIS IS MY YEAR, I THINK
  GIRLS.
GONNA SHINE
  BRENDA.
THIS IS MY SECOND CHANCE

GIRLS.
GONNA SHINE
  BRENDA.
SHOULD I WEAR BLUE OR PINK?
  GIRLS.
GONNA SHINE
  BRENDA.
SHOULD I . . .
    TOMMY. That's it, girls, dance! Okay ladies, that's lookin' nice.
    BRENDA. Nice won't do, it's gotta be perfect!
    GIRLS.
GON-NA
SHINE!
    TOMMY. One and two and three and four.
    GIRLS. One and two and three and four!
    ALL.
SHINE!

(*The SHINE montage ends. Light change. It's the end of a gruel-
    ling day. GIRLS start to vacate the multi-purpose room. As
    they do, we overhear snatches of conversation:*)

    PATTI-LYNN. God, somebody get me into a hot shower.
    DORIA. Robin, you weren't that bad. You're just nervous. It'll
wear off.
    ROBIN. I just didn't have anything to say. No offense, but I'm
not all that impressed with their shopping center.

[MUSIC #7 *DEAR MOM* #2]

    DORIA. Was it really dumb to say that?
    ROBIN. No, it was good, I think. It was the kind of thing you're
supposed to say, but . . . Oh, skip it.
    DORIA. You'll feel better after you shower. (*DORIA exits.
Alone, ROBIN sings a postcard home. Off to one side, two other
girls, SHAWN and VALERIE, gossip quietly.*)
    ROBIN.
DEAR MOM
GUESS I'VE BLOWN MY NEW CAREER MOM
GOT OFF ON A LOUSY FOOT AS A CONTESTANT
SCARED OF PUBLIC SPEAKING

COULDN'T MAKE THE WORDS UP
SILLY, HUH?
  VALERIE. Thought I was gonna lose my lunch. I heard she gave
the musical director a pinata.
  SHAWN. She is too gross. How many girls here? And I'm stuck
rooming with the Tijuana brass.
  ROBIN.
WELL, MOM
THEY KEEP US BUSIER THAN HELL MOM
HAVEN'T MADE IT TO THE HOME OF LUTHER
  BURBANK

GUESS THE PLACE'LL KEEP
GIVE THE CAT A SCRATCH FOR ME
I'VE GOTTA GET SOME SLEEP
LOVE, ROBIN
  SHAWN. I saw her rehearsing her talent act.
  VALERIE. Good huh?
  SHAWN. Not just that. Ethnic's hot stuff these days. It's just not
fair.
  VALERIE. Come on.
  SHAWN. I'm serious. Fifteen minority kids from my school got
state scholarships this year. There've been two black Miss Amer-
icas, if you count Vanessa, and the Japanese are taking over
Detroit. I wish I was disadvantaged or Jewish or something.
  VALERIE. Wow. I guess you're not interested in winning Miss
Congeniality.
  SHAWN. I'm interested in winning, period.

[MUSIC #8 *BOB'S SONG*]

*(Lights dim on them and come up in the office area, where BIG
  BOB and the judges have been meeting. A coffee urn. Empty
  styrofoam cups. BIG BOB sits on the edge of the desk, reading
  aloud from the Young American Miss handbook. His tone is
  hushed and reverential. These words mean alot to him. It's
  about ten-thirty at night. The mood is intimate, reflective,
  almost lyrical.)*

  BIG BOB. (*reading*) "That is the best part of beauty which a
picture cannot express.' We are looking for beauty, but that

which includes a natural beauty that shines through in everything this young lady says and does. In short, select a girl you would be proud to have as your own daughter." (*He closes the book. The judges murmur approval and begin to leave for the evening. As they do, BIG BOB shakes hands and speaks to them:*) Okay, folks, I guess that about covers it. We'll see the first contestant at ten A.M. tomorrow, and we'll keep calling 'em in, one by one, throughout the day. (*One of the judges, ED, has lingered in the room.*)

JUDGE (ED). I don't know, Big Bob, it's some responsibility.

BIG BOB. (*drawing the last cup of coffee from the urn*) Sure is, Ed. I can't help but think about that Miss America thing and wonder if I would've let a girl like that slip through myself. It's easy to be blinded by physical beauty.

ED. That's what I mean. Why do we bother, Bob?

BIG BOB. Why do we bother? This might sound silly but just between us, Ed, sometimes I wonder about this world of ours. Yeah, I do. You know, the recreational vehicle business isn't always as glamorous and exciting as it looks to you folks on the outside. You push and you push and you hustle to close the deal to the point where sometimes . . . Look—

YOU TOSS YER DAYS AWAY TO MAKE YER DOLLAR
AND BY THE TIME YOU BRING IT HOME
YOU KNOW, IT'S SPENT
YA DRINK YER BEER AND WATCH YER MONDAY
   FOOTBALL
AND WONDER WHERE IN HELL
YER YOUTH AND GOOD TIMES WENT

BUT MISTER, YOU CAN'T SIT AROUND
JUST FEELING SORRY FOR YOURSELF
YOU GOTTA GET ON OUT AND PITCH ON IN
AND HELP SOMEBODY ELSE . . .
RUN A CARWASH FOR THE HANDICAPPED

RAISE FUNDS FOR THE NEW TOWN HALL
SPEND A WEEKEND WITH THE LITTLE LEAGUE
TEACH A KID HOW TO PLAY BALL
SO IF YOUR OLD LIFE AIN'T EVERYTHING
YOU WANTED IT TO BE
SOMEONE ELSE'S LIFE IS BETTER
AND THAT SOUNDS GOOD TO ME.

It does something to you, Ed, spending time with these wonderful kids. Listening to their dreams . . . their aspirations . . . their beliefs . . . You come out feeling—I don't know—clean, or something. They mean that much to me, Ed. These five days every summer. They're the best part of my life.

ED. I guess so. 'Night Bob.

BIG BOB. 'Night, buddy. (*ED exits. Alone, BIG BOB sings quietly:*)
CAME HOME FROM NAM AND FOUND THE
    CIRCLES STARTED
I TURNED AROUND I HAD A CAR, A KID, A WIFE
BEFORE I KNEW IT, THERE'S A LOAN AND THEN
    A MORTGAGE
AND THEN A BUSINESS AND A RANCH HOUSE
    AND A LIFE
THAT'S NOT A LIFE

BUT MISTER, I WON'T SIT AROUND
JUST FEELIN' SORRY FOR M'SELF
NOSSIR, I'LL PITCH RIGHT IN AND GET ON OUT
AND HELP SOMEBODY ELSE
RUN A CARWASH FOR THE HANDICAPPED
RAISE FUNDS FOR THE NEW TOWN HALL
SPEND A WEEKEND WITH THE LITTLE LEAGUE
TEACH A KID HOW TO PLAY BALL
AND IF I'LL NEVER GET TO SEE THE WORLD
I HOPED I'D LIVE TO SEE
I'LL HELP SOMEONE ELSE TO GET THERE . . .
(*picks up the manual and reads:*) "The pageant is first and foremost a celebration of the ideals, values, and strength of character that ensure this nation's future."
AND THAT SOUNDS GOOD . . .
TO ME.

(*Lights dim on BIG BOB and shift to the dark multi-purpose room where LITTLE BOB is lurking, waiting for someone. After a moment, another boy his age enters.*)

FREDDY. Hey, Little Bob!

LITTLE BOB. Sshh. Jesus Christ, Freddy. Do you think you're late enough or anything?

FREDDY. I had trouble getting out of the house.

LITTLE BOB. Douchebag. Have you got the camera?

FREDDY. Of course.

LITTLE BOB. Great. The dorms are upstairs and that's where they mostly get naked. I've staked it out on this map my Dad had of the whole building and I think I've got the perfect spot. Plenty of light, completely hidden, and we'll get a birdseye view of everything.

FREDDY. If we get caught our ass . . .

LITTLE BOB. Is grass. But I don't plan to get caught. Look, it's like my Dad says, in business you have to weigh the risks against the possible gains and proceed like a man.

FREDDY. That's business. I just wanna see a little heinie.

LITTLE BOB. I can see all of that I want in Penthouse. We're talking bucks here, Freddy. Big bucks. [MUSIC #9 *NERVES*] Six dollars for rear shots, eight for full frontals . . . and fifteen if we can get anything with two girls touching. I've already got seventy-eight dollars-worth of orders.

(*Blackout. Music. When lights restore, it's early the next morning. One by one, bleary-eyed, half-asleep GIRLS begin to straggle onstage. In sharp contrast to them, we hear a chipper BRENDA on a loudspeaker:*)

BRENDA. (*V.O.*) Good morning ladies. It's six A.M. Outa your beds and into the showers. Please take a minimum of time with hair and makeup this morning—we'll understand. Today is judge's conference day and it's what's inside that counts. (*The GIRLS begin to sing as they sleepily gather for their day. Some are still in bathrobes and curlers.*)

HEIDI.

I WOKE UP STIFF

DANA.

I WOKE UP SORE

GINA.

MY BACK FEELS LIKE IT JUST CAME THROUGH
THE THIRD WORLD WAR

CONNIE-SUE.

MY THROAT IS RAW. IT FEELS LIKE STREP.

PATTI-LYNN.

I CAN'T REMEMBER YESTERDAY, NOT ONE
DAMNED STEP.

Was it toss two kick or kick two toss?
  SANDRA-KAY.
I'VE GOT SPLIT ENDS. NO WONDER SINCE
I HAVEN'T HAD A SECOND TO GO BUY CREAM RINSE
  COOKIE.
WILL THEY LET UP? WHEN WILL THEY STOP?
  HEIDI.
AND GIVE A GIRL A BREAK, A CHANCE TO
  BREATHE AND SHOP?
  ALL.
HIP HIP HOORAY. WE MEET THE JUDGES TODAY.
  CONNIE-SUE.
BUT NOTHING BUDGES TODAY—
  DANA.
I AM SO BEAT.
  HEIDI. What do you want to be when you grow up, dear?
  GINA. Asleep.
  ALL.
ANCHORS AWAY. THEY INTERVIEW US TODAY
  COOKIE.
AND TRY TO SCREW US TODAY!
  CONNIE-SUE.
OKAY, LET'S EAT
I hope they got pancakes.

(*Lights come up on OTHER GIRLS at a breakfast table in the multi-purpose room:*)

  TRUDI. Guess again.
IT'S POWDERED EGGS
  KIMBERLY.
I HATE THAT GOO.
  KATE.
I WOKE UP WITH MY PERIOD
  VALERIE.
OF COURSE. ME TOO.
  DEBRALEE.
THIS OATMEAL'S COLD
  TRUDI.
THIS BACON'S DAMP
  KIMBERLY.
THEY FED US BETTER STUFF THAN THIS AT GIRL
  SCOUT CAMP.

ALL. (*as MARIA, bright-eyed and bushy-tailed, passes by with a bowl of guacamole*)
AND SOMEONE'S UP THERE MAKING GUACAMOLE, MASHING AVOCADOS SINCE LATE LAST NIGHT!
VALERIE.
SHE'S GONNA WIN THE CROWN WITH AVOCADOS
SHAWN.
I REALLY DOUBT IT . . . SHE'S NOT WHITE.
BRENDA. Ladies. Carol's passing out the day's schedule complete with your private judges interview appointments. You've been scheduled at random, not alphabetically. Oh girls — isn't it all exciting?

(*By now, ALL GIRLS onstage are dressed, ready for the day, and gathered outside BIG BOB and BRENDA's office, where the JUDGES await the first Private Interview.*)

PATTI-LYNN.
YEAH, I'M JUST THRILLED
CONNIE-SUE.
I THINK I'LL BURST
DORIA.
OH GOD, I'M GONNA KILL MYSELF. THEY PUT ME FIRST.
ALL.
MY HAIR'S STILL WET; MY BRAIN'S STILL NUMB, BUT SOMEONE TELL THE LIONS, HERE THE
  CHRISTIANS COME
NERVES!
BIG BOB. (*poking his head out of the office*) Okay Brenda, we'll start calling the girls in now . . .
GIRLS.
I'VE GOT NERVES . . .
BRENDA. Doria Hudson, please . . .
GIRLS.
I'M ALL NERVES . . .
ROBIN. Good luck.
GIRLS. (*as DORIA nervously makes her way into the office*)
A WALKING, TALKING, BALKING BUNDLE OF
  NERVES!

(*Music ends. Outside the office, GIRLS take seats to await their*

*turn in the hotseat. Lights crossfade to inside the office, where
the grilling of DORIA is in progress:*)

BIG BOB. Doria, I see here that you helped organize a carwash
for the Clean Air Fund. Is that your favorite Charity?
DORIA. Oh, I'm in favor of all charities. But I think clean air is
really important.
JUDGE ED. Then you disagree with the President's deregula-
tion program?
DORIA. His what?
WOMAN JUDGE. Doria, why don't you tell us about your plans
for after high school? In your own words.
DORIA. Well . . . I think the most important thing in life is
helping others. (*beat*) So I'd like to be a model and work with the
mentally retarded. (*Lights crossfade. Outside the office:*)
BRENDA. Sandra-Kay MacAffee. You're next, dear. What a
lovely sweater. Is it hand-knit?
SANDRA-KAY. Yes ma'am. I did it myself.
BRENDA. Lovely.
ROBIN. (*as DORIA emerges from the office*) How'd it go?
DORIA. Great . . . I think.
ROBIN. I'm terrified.
DORIA. Just remember to mention you don't have a Dad.
ROBIN. I told you . . .
DORIA. Do it, Rob. (*Crossfade to office:*)
JUDGE ED. Sandra-Kay, what would you say is the single most
important issue facing American women today?
SANDRA-KAY. Gee, that's hard. But if I had to choose, I guess
I'd say the economy, nuclear weapons, and international
terrorism.
WOMAN JUDGE. Sandra-Kay, what is your opinion of the
Equal Rights Amendment? In your own words.
SANDRA-KAY. Well, in many ways I think it's a good thing.
But in many ways I think it's not such a good thing. I mean, we all
believe in equal pay for equal work. But, in my opinion, true
liberation comes from inside of a person.
BIG BOB. And your plans for after High School?
SANDRA-KAY. I'll probably be a nurse. I think helping others is
the most valuable and fulfilling way a person can use their life.
BIG BOB. Thank you, Sandra-Kay.
SANDRA-KAY. Thank you.
BIG BOB. (*soon as she's gone*) She's very articulate.

JUDGE ED. And that hair. (*Outside the office:*)

BRENDA. Robin—you can go in now. (*beat as ROBIN hesitantly starts in*) And then Maria, you're . . . Maria, what is that dear?

MARIA. (*as SHAWN listens in disbelief*) Oh, I thought the judges might be hungry after working so hard to help us, so I made them a specialty of my native land . . . homemade . . .

BRENDA. Guacamole dip.

MARIA. Si.

BRENDA. Like you did for the Lions Club.

MARIA. Si. You like to try?

BRENDA. Another time. (*and to the office, one last time*)

WOMAN JUDGE. Robin, I notice you work part time at J.C. Penney's, yet manage to keep your 4.0 average. Do you find it difficult to work and still get good grades?

ROBIN. Of course.

PRIEST JUDGE. (*a plainclothesman*) What would you do if your best friend was unwed and pregnant?

ROBIN. Excuse me?

PRIEST JUDGE. Would you advise her to have the baby or seek an abortion?

ROBIN. Oh . . . Well. I did alot of thinking on that subject when our county had a referendum on the Right to Life issue. I read alot of things and my Mom and I discussed it.

PRIEST JUDGE. And what did you decide?

ROBIN. I decided I was glad I wasn't old enough to vote.

BIG BOB. That's a good answer, Father. (*beat*) Say, Robin, I've noticed you've been a flute-ist for nine years.

ROBIN. I love the flute. I'm going to play it in the pageant.

WOMAN JUDGE. Why do you like to play the flute dear? In your own words.

ROBIN. Oh—lots of reasons. It sounds so pretty. And when I do it right, it sort of fills me up. I guess I like being in the spotlight, too.

BIG BOB. And you must be pleased as punch making all those other people happy.

[MUSIC #10 *RAMP SCENE*]

GIRLS.
NERVES
ROBIN. Pardon me?

GIRLS.
I'VE GOT NERVES
BIG BOB. (*trying to cue her*) The people who are listening?
GIRLS.
I'M ALL NERVES
ROBIN. (*picking it up*) Oh, yes. I think my music is one of the best ways I can help others.
BIG BOB. Very true. Is there anything else you'd like to tell us about yourself, dear? Your background . . . your family . . .
GIRLS.
A WALKING
TALKING
BALKING BUNDLE OF . . .
ROBIN. No . . . Thank you very much.

(*Button down with light on ROBIN. Then Blackout. In darkness we hear a cheer:*)

GIRLS' VOICES.
HEY! HEY! HEY! HEY!
WE'RE THE GIRLS FROM CALIFORNIA
HEAR US SCREAM AND SHOUT
WE'RE THE ONES THE BEACHBOYS
WROTE THOSE NIFTY SONGS ABOUT!

(*When Lights restore, we are on the bare stage of the auditorium where the Pageant itself will take place. The GIRLS are rehearsing — running on a semi-circular ramp that extends out into the audience. TOMMY supervises.*)

GIRLS.
YOUNG AND AMERICAN, YOUNG AND AMERICAN!
WORDS WE CAN SAY WITH SUCH PRIDE . . .
TOMMY. Keep it moving, ladies, KEEP IT MOVING! Close it up there, Debralee!

(*BIG BOB enters and surveys the scene with approval. After a moment, BRENDA enters and rushes past him. She carries a roll of blueprint-style drawings and seems more agitated than we imagined she could ever allow herself to be.*)

BIG BOB. Hey, how's it goin', sweetheart?

BRENDA. Not too well. Mr. French, if I could speak to you—

TOMMY. In a minute.

BRENDA. Mr. French . . . It's about this runway you had built. Thank goodness Carol brought it to my attention. It wasn't in the plans you mailed us and—

TOMMY. I always do a runway.

BRENDA. Yes, but—

TOMMY. You can't stage a beauty show without it.

BRENDA. But it wasn't in the plans, you see. It isn't on these drawings.

BIG BOB. (*taking the roll of drawings from BRENDA*) May I see those?

BRENDA. Mr. French, could I have your attention please?

TOMMY. Okay. Five.

BRENDA. We're talking about a great deal of money here.

TOMMY. I thought we were talking about a runway.

BRENDA. Which obliterates the first ten rows of the orchestra —one hundred seats. We call those seats the Golden Circle, Mr. French. They cost ten dollars each—two dollars more than the regular tickets—and we've sold them all.

TOMMY. What do you expect me to do?

BRENDA. Well—I'm sorry, but . . . you'll have to take out that ramp.

TOMMY. And re-stage everything.

BRENDA. I'm sure it's not impossible.

BIG BOB. (*He's found something in the plans.*) Brenda—

TOMMY. You bet it is impossible. These girls ain't Ginger Rogers.

BIG BOB. Brenda, it's here. You musta missed it, honey, cause it's here. Addendum to page three. Right in Mr. French's plans. A ramp. A runway.

TOMMY. Of course it's there. Mrs. Freelander it's not my fault if you didn't notice to allow for it in your budget and it's way too late to do anything about it now. These girls are barely squeaking by as-is. To take that runway out not only isn't fair, it isn't safe.

BIG BOB. It is late, Brenda.

BRENDA. Well there is another solution I suppose.

TOMMY. And what's that?

BRENDA. (*The iron lady surfaces.*) Let's see, one hundred seats at ten apiece comes to one thousand dollars. We could withhold that from your check.

TOMMY. (*Beat. Then softly:*) Well, well, well. Sugar and spice

and everything nice. (*Beat, shouted to a stagehand upstage:*)
Strike the ramp. Tony, can I see you, please . . . (*TOMMY crosses upstage to address TONY.*)

BRENDA. (*to BIG BOB, quiet but livid*) And thank you very much.

TOMMY. Ladies, I've got an announcement.

(*We don't hear his announcement. Just the girls' disappointed group reaction to it. As the BRENDA/BOB scene continues, we see but do not hear TOMMY upstage, explaining how he'll re-stage routines without the runway.*)

BIG BOB. I'm just concerned about the girls.

BRENDA. We'd look like fools without a Golden Circle.

BIG BOB. We could explain. We made a mistake.

BRENDA. (*bursting*) And they don't give a . . . hang about mistakes in Baton Rouge. They want it perfect. I want perfect. I demand it of myself and I am proud that others ask it of me.

BIG BOB. Honey —

BRENDA. Don't.

BIG BOB. Please. Talk to me.

BRENDA. No. Let's forget it. Didn't happen. Gone.

BIG BOB. Come here.

BRENDA. I've got a headache. (*exit*)

TOMMY. Okay. Lemme have the Aqua color group. Just the Aqua color group. Peach Group, you're on break. But stay close. Five six seven eight . . .

(*BOB exits. Upstage, a group of GIRLS begins the re-staging rehearsal with TOMMY. Downstage, ROBIN and DORIA are among the GIRLS on break.*)

GIRLS.
YOUNG AND AMERICAN, YOUNG AND
    AMERICAN . . .
ROBIN. I'm totally confused. I can't believe he's changing it.
DORIA. You'll do fine.
ROBIN. This all seems to come so natural to you.
DORIA. Yeah? Yeah. Oh God, do I wish this was televised. God do I wish this got back home. Joe and Betty'd eat their words.
ROBIN. Joe and Betty?
DORIA. My Mom and step-Dad.

DORIA. I mean I'm no great shakes at school, but jeez, I won my local pageant, right? You'd think they'd like be proud or something. Well who cares, you know? This is my year Rob, I can feel it. Taste it. Oh God, I want to win so bad.

(*From the rehearsal upstage, we hear a shout from one of the GIRLS. She has turned an ankle and fallen. The rehearsal stops and everyone gathers around her.*)

TOMMY. Okay, honey, just relax. Don't crowd her, ladies. Give her some air.

BIG BOB. (*re-enters*) What happened, what just happened? Oh my God.

TONY. She tripped or something. I didn't see.

KIMBERLY. It's just we're used to dancing on the ramp.

KATE. There's not room enough up here.

BRENDA. Let me through. She's fine. She's fine. Carol—

HEIDI. It hurts.

BRENDA. Set an example for the others, dear. Carol, get . . .

CAROL. (*prompting*) Heidi . . .

BRENDA. Get Heidi to my office. She'll need an ace bandage, a Pepsi, and a chance to calm down. Okay, everybody, let's not over-react. Heidi's fine. Keep smiling. Keep working. (*on her way off*) Bob, make sure it wasn't a nail she tripped on, nothing we can be sued for.

TOMMY. (*who overhears this*) What touching concern. (*beat*) I'm putting it back. And tell your wife to deduct the thousand from my check. You hear that everybody? The ramp stays in. Tony—tell your guys to hustle. Lemme see the Aqua color group. Peach on break. Five six seven eight . . .

[MUSIC #11 *YOUNG AND AMERICAN*]

BIG BOB. Mr. French—(*Music begins. The GIRLS start their runway routine.*)

BIG BOB. Mr. French—my wife's been under pressure and . . .

TOMMY. We've all been under pressure. Keep it moving, ladies. Close it up behind Marie. Keep it moving, keep it . . .

(*As the GIRLS begin running in choreographed formation, there is a light change. A sign flies in reading WELCOME TO*

*YOUNG AMERICAN MISS PRELIMINARY COMPETI-
TION. The sound of the rehearsal piano is replaced by that of
an orchestra. A group of red, white, and blue costumed
GIRLS runs onstage. It is clear now that time has passed.
We're watching Preliminary Competitions and the GIRLS
are performing for real:*)

GIRLS.
YOUNG AND AMERICAN, YOUNG AND AMERICAN
WORDS WE CAN SAY WITH SUCH PRIDE
WE'VE GOT THE KEYS TO THE FUTURE
AND WE'RE UNLOCKIN' IT
RUN OUT AND BUY STOCK IN IT
LIKE GERRY FERRARO, WE GIRLS OF TOMORROW
ARE READY TO PROMISE YOU THIS
WE'LL GET THINGS THRIVIN'
SO RELAX AND LEAVE THE DRIVIN'
TO A YOUNG AMERICAN MISS

NO DON'T DESPAIR,
EVEN WHEN RECESSION'S IN THE AIR
IF THERE'S A DEPRESSION, WE'LL BE THERE
WE'LL BE SMILIN' THROUGH IT,
SO FORGET THE NASTY OLD NATIONAL DEBT

WE'RE ON HAND
WITH A DEMONSTRATION THAT WE'VE PLANNED
PROVIN' TO THE NATION THAT IF WE CAN DO
   THIS FOR YOU
WE'VE GOT THE MOXIE TO
RUN THIS GREAT BIG LAND
WE'RE GONNA JUMP, SHAKE A LEG AND SHOW
PRESIDENT REAGAN NO
NEED FOR THE COUNTRY TO FEAR
NOTHIN' AT ALL WE CAN'T HANDLE
YOUNG AMERICA'S HERE!
   BIG BOB. (*enters and addresses the audience*) Hey, it's great to
see a turnout like this. I'm Big Bob Freelander, Dean of Judges for
this year's Pageant and . . . uh . . . well . . . (*reads from a
card*) On Preliminary Night a thrilling carnival atmosphere pre-
vails as the girls compete in the categories of Vim and Vigor,
Individual Athletic Skill, Grace and Poise, Scholastic Achieve-

ment, and of course, my personal favorite, Creative Talent. All
leading up to the evening's grand finale, when winners are an-
nounced for this year's Outstanding Achievement Awards. And
so without further ado . . . let's proceed to Category Number
One . . . The Vim and Vigor Competition! Take it away,
girls . . .

*(Music swells and GIRLS come bounding onstage to perform
aerobic routines. Two groups of eight each. BIG BOB and the
JUDGES wander amongst the GIRLS, taking notes on each
one's performance. When the routines are finished, the
GIRLS perform a little dance routine to the following:)*

GIRLS.
WE'LL MATCH THE GUYS
KEEPIN' FIT WITH
  HEALTHY
EXERCISE
WE'LL BE HANGIN'
  TOUGH
WITH OUR ALLIES
IF WE EVER GOTTA GO
  TO WAR

GIRLS.
YA BETTER BETCHA
WE'RE MATCHIN' THE
  GUYS
AMAZIN' ARMS
IN-CA-RED-IBLE THIGHS
BRING ON THE COMMIES,
WE'LL CUT 'EM TO SIZE

THE LADIES'LL EVEN THE
  SCORE
BUT TAKE HEART
WE WON'T LET THE
  PLANET
BLOW APART
IF A JANE OR JANET IS AS
STRONG AS A HERCULES
YOU CAN JUST BETCHA
  SHE'S
ALSO PLENTY SMART

WE'LL SAVE THE PLANET

WE WISH WE RAN IT

*(Several GIRLS enter for a College Bowl-style quiz competition.
ROBIN is among them. BIG BOB is the quizmaster.)*

BIG BOB. Category Two. The Scholastic Achievement Quiz.
Question One. In Computer Basic, the purpose of the PEEK
function is to read data from a specified memory location. The
purpose of the POKE function is to . . .

TRUDI. WRITE data to a specified memory location!

BIG BOB. Right! This 1964 Presidential Candidate is the author of "Conscience of a Conservative" . . .

PATTI-LYNN. Barry Goldwater!

BIG BOB. Right! This German philosopher wrote Beyond Good and Evil.

DANA. Arnold Schwartzenegger?

BIG BOB. Wrong.

ROBIN. Frederick Nietzsche?

BIG BOB. Right! Well that concludes our Scholastic Quiz. And now let's go to Category Three!

GIRLS.

HOT DOG! OH BOY!

IT'S TIME FOR TALENT!

WE SING AND DANCE AND ACT AND HOW!

ALL YOUNG AMERICA'S GOT TALENT!

AS WE WILL PROVE RIGHT NOW!

BIG BOB. Presenting Bakersfield's Young American Miss, Sandra-Kay MacAffee and her friend Jerry . . .

(SANDRA-KAY enters and performs a ventriloquism act with her dummy, Jerry.)

DUMMY.

YOU KNOW IT AIN'T ALOTTA FUN TO BE A DUMMY

SANDRA-KAY. Whatdya mean?

DUMMY.

I MEAN A DUMMY HAS A REALLY CRUMBY LIFE

SANDRA-KAY. Explain that, please.

DUMMY.

I SIT HERE ON YOUR KNEE

AND YOU SAY EVERYTHING FOR ME

IT ISN'T FAIR, YOU'RE JUST MY OWNER NOT MY WIFE

SANDRA-KAY. Oh, please.

DUMMY.

I'D RATHER GO TO WORK FOR SHARI LEWIS

SANDRA-KAY. Wait a minute —

JERRY, THAT'S A VERY NASTY THING TO SAY

DUMMY.

IF I HAD LEGS I'D UP AND SPLIT

SANDRA-KAY.

THAT'S FINE, YOU'RE FIRED,

DUMMY.
NO, I QUIT
  SANDRA-KAY.
OKAY
  DUMMY.
OKAY
  SANDRA-KAY.
OKAY
  DUMMY.
OKAY
  SANDRA-KAY.
OKAY
  DUMMY.
OKAY
  GIRLS.
SEE WHAT WE MEAN,
WE'VE ALL GOT TALENT!
(YOUNG AND AMERICAN!)

  BIG BOB. And here's Carson, California's Young American Miss. Miss Cookie Wilson!

(*COOKIE enters to sing Gospel:*)

  COOKIE.
EZEKIAL SAW THE WHEEL
DOWN BY THE GRAPES OF WRATH AND SO
NOW ALL GOD'S CHILDREN, WE GOT SHOES
SWEET CHARIOT, SWING LOW
GET THEE BE-HIND ME, SATAN
DON'T YOU DARE COME NEAR
YOU BAD OLD UG-LY DEVIL, YOU
GET OUT OF HERE
LOOKOUT YOU SINNERS, LOOKOUT BELOW!

  BIG BOB. And now—on point—with her amazing flaming batons. Here's Visalia's Young American Miss, Connie-Sue Whipple. (*CONNIE performs with flaming Fire Batons.*) And with a musical . . . cooking demonstration, Salinas' Young American Miss. Maria Gonzales.

(*MARIA enters and begins her talent act, which consists of singing and dancing as she simultaneously prepares a Mexican feast: gazpacho, tacos, and flan.*)

MARIA.
IN THE U. S. OF A. I SEE, LATELY,
THE CUISINE OF MY COUNTRY DOES WELL
SI, THEY'RE HAVING IT MY WAY
ON EVERY BIG HIGHWAY
WHAT SIGN DO YOU SEE? TACO BELL!

NOW MARIA, SHE'LL TELL YOU THE REASON
SEE, US MEXICAN GIRLS ARE SO SMART
AND IF WE WANT AN HOMBRE TO WRITE DOWN
   OUR NOMBRE
OUR FOOD IS THE WAY TO HIS HEART.

SERVE A BEEF ENCHILADA
FULL OF CARNE PICADA
HE'LL SAY "THANK YOU", DE NADA
MAKE SURE THERE'S A WAD A
FRIED BEANS ON THE SIDE

NEXT YOU GIVE HIM GAZPACHO
NICE AND HOT, 'CAUSE HE'S MACHO
FINISH OFF WITH SOME FLAN
AND I PROMISE YOUR MAN
HE WILL MAKE YOU HIS BRIDE!

YOU WANNA KEEP YOUR LOVE ALIVE?
YOU BAKE THIS AT THREE TWENTY-FIVE!

YOU WANNA REALLY MAKE HIM SCREAM?
YOU GARNISH THIS WITH SOUR CREAM

FOR DESSERT I RECRUIT A
ENSALATA DE FRUTA
PIÑA, FRESAS, Y COCO
THEY DRIVE THE BOYS LOCO
NO JOKE-O! OLE!
WHEN YOU COOK LIKE MARIA
LOVE IS SWEET AS SANGRIA
SO WHIP UP A TORTILLA
HE'LL GET THE IDEA
AND COME ROUND TO SEE YA
DOWN MEXICO WAY!

GIRLS.
WE'VE ALL BEEN BLESSED WITH GOLDEN TALENT!
(YOUNG AND AMERICAN!)

BIG BOB. And with an inspirational dramatic recitation she has written by herself here is Yuba City's Young American Miss . . . Doria Hudson. (*DORIA, in an elaborate gay nineties costume, dramatically recites in time to music by Beethoven:*)

DORIA.
Fashion. How I followed that.
Beauty's gilded copycat.
Spangled dresses, floppy hat,
And jewels, I had them too.
But one day, on a shopping spree,
Across the street—I chanced to see
A building, and it called to me.
It was of course . . . a *li-bra-ry.*
(*She approaches a podium and solemnly picks up a volume of Shakespeare.*)
To thine own self be true.
(*She looks up at us in awe and wonder, then portentously closes the book.*)
At last I'd found a beauty aid.
That isn't painted on or sprayed.
Simplicity. My choice was made.
I knew what I must do.
(*She begins what amounts to a chaste and ceremonious striptease, reciting as she goes:*)
Off came the silly shoes, the dress,
And all that glittering foolishness . . .
The costume jewels, the hat, the curls,
The silly rhinestone pin.
(*Finished with the disrobing, she stands before us now in a simple, form-fitting white leotard and tights.*)
When finished with this task was I,
No more a spangled butterfly
I'd learned at last one must rely
On beauty from within
(*She approaches the podium, opens a Bible and reads:*)
Consider the lilies of the field,
How they grow. They work not. They toil not.
(*She takes the two calla lilies from the vase . . .*)
Yet I say unto you that even Solomon

In all his glory . . .
Was not one half so beautiful . . .
(*and crosses them under her breasts*)
As these.
GIRLS.
COME A-LONG!
JOIN IN AND SING A GEORGE M. COHAN SONG
YA KNOW YOUR GIRLS'D NEVER STEER YA WRONG
SING OUT STRONG
WE'RE YANKEE DOODLE, THE KIT AND CABOODLE,
WE'RE YOUNG AND AMERICAN, YOUNG AND
    AMERICAN
LEADERS OF CHEERS AND OF MEN
WE COULD TAKE OVER TOMORROW
YESSIR WE'RE TOUGH ENOUGH
WE CAN HANDLE GORBACHOV
WE'RE YOUNG AND AMERICAN, YOUNG AND
    AMERICAN
HOLD OUT UNTIL THE DAY WHEN
YOUTH WILL BE SERVED AND START SERVING
GLOWING AND TAN
MOVE OVER, MAN
WE'VE GOT A PLAN
TIME WE BEGAN
CAUSE WE'RE YOUNG AND A-MER-I-CAN!

(*Drumroll. The GIRLS are all gathered onstage. BIG BOB enters
to announce the night's winners:*)

BIG BOB. For outstanding Achievement in The Vim and Vigor
Category . . . Sandra Kay MacAffee, Bakersfield's Young
American Miss. (*SANDRA-KAY comes forward to
accept . . . jumping up and down, crying, hugging, over-
whelmed.*) This year's Scholastic Achievement
Award . . . Robin Gibson. Antelope Valley's Young American
Miss. (*Dazed, she comes forward.*) And now . . . for Outstanding Achievement in the Individual Talent Category . . . (*A
moment of silence. Spot on DORIA. She holds her breath.*) Maria
Gonzales . . . Salinas' Young American Miss. (*MARIA
squeals with glee and comes forward. BIG BOB awkardly emu-
lates a TV host and closes the night's events as a scrim comes
down, representing the auditorium curtain.*) That's all for Prelim-

inaries, folks. But I know we'll see you tomorrow night for the real
show . . . The Big One. California's Young American Miss
Pageant, hosted by World Famous NBC Radio Personality and
Syndicated Columnist . . . California's Sunshine Boy, Ted
Farley. God Bless and Goodnight.

(*Bleeding through the scrim, we see the GIRLS backstage, immediately following the Preliminary proceedings. There's a lot of
hugging, crying, gossiping going on in the background. But
we focus on SHAWN, who is ranting at VALERIE.*)

SHAWN. I just can't believe it. What are they, crazy? Blind?
They call that talent? That Happy Latin Homemaker shit? How
could they give it to her? (*SHAWN stalks off, furious. Now we
focus on DORIA, who is very upset. ROBIN tries to comfort her.*)
    ROBIN. She told me. A lot of girls who don't win anything
Preliminary Night go on to win the contest. Talent's only part
of . . .
    DORIA. It was my best shot, Rob. If they didn't like me taking
off my clothes, it's a cinch they're gonna hate my grades.

(*DORIA bursts into tears and runs offstage. ROBIN follows. We
focus now on BRENDA, pushing through the crowd toward
BIG BOB, who is downstage near the ramp, removing his tie.
She leads a tall, imposing, corporate, impeccably dressed,
white-haired gentleman. This is DALE WILSON-SHEARS.
And there is a little of Jerry Falwell peeking through his
carefully cultivated charm.*)

BRENDA. Bob, Bob . . . (*She reaches him.*) Robert, this is
Mr. Wilson-Shears. Our National Chairman.
    WILSON-SHEARS. Fine job, Mr. Freelander.
    BIG BOB. We try, sir. You know, the Santa Rosa Jaycees are
proud and honored to have you here.
    WILSON-SHEARS. It's a pleasure. Your California State Pag-
eant and your wife's work in particular have a reputation for
excellence. I'm looking forward to . . . (*beat*) Say, that ramp
extends out quite a few rows, doesn't it?
    BIG BOB. Well yessir, it does. You see —
    WILSON-SHEARS. The State Pageants don't usually use those.
How do you handle the Golden Circle?
    BRENDA. May I explain, sir? You see, Mr. French felt it was

artistically important to have a ramp. Well, I explained we count on the money from those Golden Circle seats and what do you think he did? After just a moment of discussion, he agreed to deduct the thousand dollars we'd lose directly from his own fee!

WILSON-SHEARS. That must have been quite a moment of discussion.

BRENDA. Not really. And the pageant did look wonderful with that ramp. Now if you'll excuse me, there's no rest for the weary this weekend. Carol—(*BRENDA exits.*)

WILSON-SHEARS. That's what the pageant's all about. Women like that.

BIG BOB. She's a dynamo. But about this ramp. You see, we didn't notice it was on the plans and by the time we caught it . . . Well, it wasn't Mr. French's fault and I've been thinking. Now, what if the Santa Rosa Jaycees paid him five hundred of that thousand dollars and your National Committee would pick up the other five . . .

WILSON-SHEARS. After your wife persuaded him to deduct it from his check?

BIG BOB. But I told you, it was our mistake.

WILSON-SHEARS. Why are you so concerned about this?

BIG BOB. Well heck, I make fundraising speeches all the time, about "Going for Gold and Forming the Future." Sportsmanship. Fairplay. We're setting an example and I think it's inconsistent to . . .

WILSON-SHEARS. That's very admirable, Mr. Freelander. I appreciate your concern for principle. And no one has higher principles than the Young American Miss Foundation. But it takes alot of money to do our worthwhile and wonderful work. Just ask the folks at the Jerry Lewis telethon. Charity's a business. Tommy my boy, terrific job. Super!

(*SHEARS exits. BIG BOB stands there a moment as SHEARS' words sink in, then starts out. As he goes, lights transporting us back to the dormitories. DORIA, on her bed, rummages in her bag and produces a pack of Marlboros. ROBIN stands in the doorway for a moment, then speaks:*)

ROBIN. What are you doing?

DORIA. What does it look like I'm doing? Now that I'm sure I'm not winning anything I might as well.

ROBIN. You shouldn't be so sure you're gonna lose.

DORIA. I always do. Like if I like a boy and he likes me somehow it ends up I'm a slut with all the 'nice' girls who don't live in mobile homes. Just ask my folks, Rob. I'm a washout, loser, bad grades, fast track . . .

ROBIN. Doria, stop it. Believe me, you're not anything you shouldn't be. You're just fine. I mean it. And you've been a real good friend. I probably would've turned around and gone home if it hadn't been for you.

DORIA. You mean it?

ROBIN. 'Course I do. It's terrible to see you do this to yourself. You know, it's just a contest.

DORIA. Just a contest. That's your problem, attitude.

ROBIN. What do you mean?

DORIA. I mean you won scholastic achievement tonight. They like you. You could win.

ROBIN. Come on.

DORIA. You could, if you'd stop goin' on how you can't dance, how you don't want to play for sympathy and tell 'em you don't have a Dad . . .

ROBIN. Let's go to bed.

DORIA. I'm serious. Okay, I blew it, I'm washed up, but you've got a real shot. God, there's so much I could teach you.

ROBIN. Like what?

DORIA. I guess I should've before but we were in competition. Okay, for starters, Robin, you've got to wear panty hose. Bare legs look splotchy under lights.

ROBIN. They do?

DORIA. Disgusting . . . and here, use this on the bottom of your leotard.

ROBIN. What's that?

DORIA. Spray glue. All the Miss Americas use it on their bathing suits to keep 'em from riding up. And Robin, you've got to smile more.

ROBIN. I've smiled til my gums are raw.

DORIA. You oughta be putting vaseline on your teeth, so your lips glide over. All the girls do it.

ROBIN. You're kidding.

DORIA. The redhead uses enough to grease a flagpole. And there's more, lots more . . . (*sings*)

[MUSIC #12 *UNTIL TOMORROW NIGHT*]

YOU DIDN'T JUMP UP AND DOWN ENOUGH
   WHEN SANDRA WON.
AND YOU DIDN'T EVEN CRY WHEN YOU WON
   YOURSELF.
THE JUDGES ARE LOOKING FOR LOTS OF EMOTION
GIVE 'EM EMOTION
   ROBIN. I'll try.
   DORIA.
WE'LL GET RID OF THOSE DUMB LITTLE BOWS
   THAT YOU WEAR,
LINE YOUR EYES WITH A LITTLE MORE WHITE,
AND WE'LL SNEAK JUST A HINT OF GOLD SPRAY
IN YOUR HAIR
SO IT SHINES WHEN IT CATCHES THE LIGHT
TOMORROW NIGHT

(*Lights lower on ROBIN and DORIA and find GIRLS in other
   rooms. They sing:*)

   SIX GIRLS.
WELL HERE IT GOES, THE TENSION MOUNTS
MY COOL IS DRAINING, OUNCE BY OUNCE
'CAUSE THIS IS THE PART
WHERE IT STARTS TO GET STRANGE HERE

(*Lights find still more girls in still other rooms.*)

   SIX MORE GIRLS.
I'M SO STRUNG OUT, I'M SO DONE IN
I HOPE IT WON'T AFFECT MY SKIN.
DON'T THINK I CAN DEAL
'CAUSE I FEEL A REAL CHANGE HERE
   FIRST SIX GIRLS.
WHAT DO THEY WANT FROM ME AND HOW CAN
   I BE IT?
   SECOND SIX GIRLS.
OR IF I *AM* IT, CAN I GET THEM TO SEE IT?
   ALL TWELVE.
I NEED A SEDATIVE
MY FINGERS SHAKE, MY BRAIN'S A SIEVE
I'VE ONLY GOT SO MUCH TO GIVE
HOW WILL I LIVE UNTIL TOMORROW NIGHT?!

GIRLS.
I SENSE A FEELING IN THIS PLACE
IT'S MAKING ME A BASKET CASE
THE STAKES ARE TOO HIGH, THEY UNNERVE
  AND UNGLUE ME

I CAN'T COOL OFF, I CAN'T RELAX
DO KIDS MY AGE HAVE HEART ATTACKS?
I'M TOO YOUNG TO DIE! WHY'S IT HAPPENING
  TO ME?

WHAT DO THEY WANT FROM ME? I'LL DO IT, I
  SWEAR IT!
JUST SAY WHAT COLOR DO THEY LIKE AND I'LL
  WEAR IT!

LOOK, THERE'S THE WINDOWSILL
I THINK I'LL JUMP . . . I WON'T . . . I WILL
WHY NOT? THERE'S NOTHING LEFT TO KILL!
MY HEART BE STILL, UNTIL TOMORROW NIGHT!

(*Lights up in the shower room. We see SHAWN, singing to VA-
    LERIE and then to herself:*)

SHAWN.
I CAN'T BELIEVE SHE WON,
CAUSE WHEN IT'S SAID AND DONE
YOU KNOW SHE REALLY DOESN'T DESERVE IT
I CAN'T BELIEVE THIS SHIT
THAT GUACAMOLE BIT
AND PEOPLE STOOD THERE WATCHIN' HER SERVE
  IT
I CAN'T BELIEVE IT WORKS
THE WAY SHE GRINS AND SMIRKS
AND THEN SHE WALKS AWAY WITH A PRIZE
I'M SEEIN' RED RIGHT NOW
I'M GONNA FIGURE HOW
TO CUT THAT SPANISH KID DOWN TO SIZE . . .
TOMORROW—

(*Light shift. We return to the dormitory. Each girl is in her own
    space, but all feeling the same thing:*)

GIRLS.
TOMORROW NIGHT THE AXE DESCENDS
WILL I GET THROUGH? WELL, THAT DEPENDS . . .
I CAN'T GET TO SLEEP, I KEEP TOSSING AND TURNING!
I KEEP REVIEWING IN MY HEAD
THE THINGS I DID, THE THINGS I SAID
I WISH I KNEW HOW MANY POINTS AM I EARNING?

WHAT DO THEY WANT FROM ME? I'LL DO IT, I
WANNA!
WHO DO THEY WANNA SEE? SNOW WHITE OR
MADONNA?

HOW HAVE I DONE SO FAR?
I WISH I LOOKED LIKE TERRI GARR
I WONDER WHAT MY CHANCES ARE
IT'S SO BIZARRE! UNTIL TOMORROW NIGHT . . .
UNTIL TOMORROW NIGHT . . .
UNTIL TOMORROW NIGHT . . .
UNTIL TOMORROW . . .

(*Lights return to SHAWN, alone now in the shower room,
    wrapped in a towel. There's a loud clank from an air-condi-
    tioning vent, then a muffled "Ouch."*)

SHAWN. Hey what the hell? (*another, quieter clank*)
    SHAWN. Is somebody in there? (*She lifts the flap-like metal
grate open to reveal a cowering LITTLE BOB and FREDDY.*)
Oh my God! What do you think you're . . . (*The BOYS crawl
out into the room.*) Jesus Christ, that's a goddam camera, isn't it?
    LITTLE BOB. Please don't tell my Dad.
    SHAWN. Your Dad? Wait a minute. I know you . . . You're
the Freelander kid.
    LITTLE BOB. No I'm not.
    FREDDY. He's not.
    SHAWN. The hell he's not.
    LITTLE BOB. Please don't tell!
    SHAWN. You bet I'm gonna tell. I'm gonna tell your father, the
police, and anybody else I can . . . That is . . . unless . . .
    LITTLE BOB. Unless what?
    SHAWN. Let's you and me have a talk.

(*We lose the shower room and lights return to the rest dormitory.
In each cubicle, nook and cranny, we discover, is a girl. And
each girl is having her own personal anxiety attack. The
movement is contained and semi-stylized as each girl strug-
gles with her own private sleeplessness.*)

GIRLS.
OH GOD IT'S BAD AND GETTING WORSE
I NEED A SHRINK, I NEED A NURSE
MY HEAD'S GONNA BLOW AND MY TUMMY
    CONVULSES

MY BREATH IS GONE, MY TEMPLES ACHE
I'M VERGING ON A NERVOUS BREAK
I DON'T WANNA KNOW WHAT THE RATE OF MY
    PULSE IS

WHAT DO THEY WANT TO SEE? A CUTE
    FUTURE-SURGEON!
A SAINT, A P.H.D, AN ATHLETE, A VIRGIN!

A GIVING, LIVING DOLL
WHO'S NOT TOO SHORT AND NOT TOO TALL
I'VE GOT TO KEEP MY WITS ON CALL AND BE IT *ALL*
UNTIL TOMORROW NIGHT

(*We add DORIA and ROBIN to the picture, downstage:*)

DORIA.
LISTEN CLOSE, ROB, AND BE SMART, ROB
YOU'VE GOT SOMETHIN' THEY SEE
I JUST KNOW, ROB, YOU COULD WIN, ROB
IF YOU LISTEN TO ME—
I'VE GOT SO MUCH TO TEACH
'BOUT YOUR WALK AND YOUR SPEECH AND
    YOUR GOWN
AND YOUR MAKE-UP, YOUR HAIR
SIT RIGHT THERE, GOT TO GET IT ALL DOWN
BY TOMORROW NIGHT—

(*All sixteen girls are onstage:*)

GIRLS.
HOW WILL I LIVE UNTIL TOMORROW COMES?
SOON AS I TURN OUT THE LIGHT—
VISIONS OF BLAZING AUDITORIUMS!
HOW WILL I GET THROUGH THE NIGHT?

(*We add BIG BOB and BRENDA in separate pools of light, downstage of the dorms.*)

BIG BOB.
OKAY, BOB, DON'T OVER-REACT
DON'T GO AND MAKE TOO MUCH OF IT,
STRESS IS A SICKNESS IN THESE SITUATIONS
WE ALL MAY HAVE A TOUCH OF IT.

BIG BOB.	BRENDA.	DORIA.
WHAT'S WITH BRENDA	EIGHTEEN YEARS AGO	
WHAT'S GOIN' ON?	YES, I'M DOING MUCH BETTER NOW	
DON'T GO AND MAKE TOO MUCH OF IT		
	AND IT'S FUNNY HOW	
STRESS IS A SICKNESS IN THESE SITUATIONS WE ALL MAY HAVE A TOUCH OF IT . . .		YOU CAN DO IT, ROB WE'LL STAY UP TIL DAWN OKAY TAKE THAT OFF OKAY PUT THIS ON

BRENDA (*con'd*).
I FEEL WIDE AWAKE
BIG BOB.
BUT SHE'S SO HIGH STRUNG
DORIA.
YOU CAN DO IT, ROB
BRENDA.
I FEEL TENSE BUT YOUNG

BIG BOB.	BRENDA.	DORIA.
I GUESS	HARDLY WAIT	ONLY GOT
MAYBE	UNTIL	UNTIL
SHE'LL	TOMORROW	TOMORROW
RELAX		
TOMORROW		

GIRLS (*over*).
I'M A TYPICAL HIGH SCHOOL SENIOR . . .
WHO'S GOT NERVES, I'VE GOT NERVES
I'M ALL NERVES, I'VE GOT NERVES . . .
  ALL.
TOMORROW NIGHT THEY TURN THE SCREWS
AND ONE WILL WIN, THE REST WILL LOSE
I'M PAYING MY DUES BUT I DON'T UNDERSTAND
  THEM
THE MESSAGES THEY SEND ARE MIXED
MY BRAIN IS BROKEN, CAN'T BE FIXED
TOMORROW THEY CHOOSE! I DON'T KNOW WHAT
  TO HAND THEM

WHAT DO THEY WANT FROM ME?
GOD KNOWS I'VE BEEN TRYING
THEY SAY RELAX AND BE YOURSELF
BUT THEY'RE LYING

SO I'M IN MORTAL FEAR
I CANNOT TAKE THIS ATMOSPHERE
I NEED A JOINT, I NEED A BEER
PLEASE SOMEONE GET ME OUTA HERE
IT'S ALL TOO MUCH, AND SO IN SUM
I'VE LOST MY EQUILIBRIUM
I FEEL SO FAT, I FEEL SO DUMB
I NEED TO KNOW THE END WILL COME IN SIGHT
IT WILL TOMORROW NIGHT
OH GOD IT WILL ALRIGHT TO-MOR-ROW
NIGHT TOMORROW NIGHT TOMORROW NIGHT
  TOMORROW NIGHT

TOMORROW . . . GOD! TO-MOR-ROW NIGHT!

(*The Curtain starts down as the GIRLS release their anxiety in a
  pillow fight.*)

CURTAIN
END ACT ONE

[MUSIC #13 *ENTR'ACTE*]

ACT TWO

[MUSIC #14 *OPENING ACT TWO*]

In her dormitory room, ROBIN sits alone, holding a yellow smile-face teeshirt. She folds it and puts it into a bag.

ROBIN.
DEAR MOM
BRINGING' HOME A SOUVENIR, MOM,
BUT IT ISN'T FROM THE HOUSE OF LUTHER BURBANK
WON'T SEE THAT, I GUESS
HARDLY SEEN THE OUTSIDE OF THIS BUILDING YET,
MUCH LESS . . .

(ROBIN finishes packing the tee-shirt and moves out of her room and downstage. As she does, her dorm room disappears and we see the pageant dressing rooms, which are already a bee-hive of activity. GIRLS are in various stages of dress and undress, some sitting at mirrors doing makeup, some running through routines, all in a state of high anxiety.)

COOKIE. (*trying to line her eyes*)
OH GOD, I'M SHAKING.
I WILL NEVER GET THIS RIGHT.
GIRLS. (*looking into mirrors, doing makeup*)
OH GOD . . .
VALERIE. (*enters, frenzied*)
WHO'S GOT AN EXTRA PAIR OF PANTYHOSE?
SANDRA-KAY.
I MIGHT.
GIRLS.
DEAR GOD . . .
CONNIE-SUE. (*trying to squeeze into a strange vest*)
I CAN'T WEAR THIS.
IT DOESN'T FIT!
HEIDI.
IT'S UPSIDE DOWN.
GINA.
OH NO! QUICK, SOMEONE HELP ME!
I SPILLED PEPSI ON MY GOWN!

65

GIRLS.
STAY CALM . . .
  SHAWN. (*to TRUDI, who is eating a Big Mac*)
HOW CAN YOU EAT THAT?
  TRUDI.
I WAS HUNGRY.
I'LL BE FINE.
  GIRLS.
STAY VERY CALM . . .
  PATTI-LYNN. (*holding up some beads*)
WHO LOST A ROSARY?
  MARIA. (*greatly relieved*)
OH GRACIAS! IT'S MINE.
  GIRLS.
SERENELY CALM
  KIMBERLY.
THIS ZIPPER'S BROKEN
  DEBRALEE.
SO IS THIS. IT DOESN'T SNAP.
  DANA. (*enters with an unwieldy arrangement of flowers*)
LOOK WHAT I GOT!
  COOKIE.
LOOKOUT!
  CONNIE-SUE.
BE CAREFUL!
  COOKIE.
CRAP!

(*The arrangement spills all over the dressing table. An oblivious
    BRENDA enters and sings cheerfully:*)

  BRENDA.
THIS YEAR
  COOKIE. Let's clean it up!
  BRENDA.
THIS IS GONNA BE THE BEST YEAR
  VALERIE. Another run!
  BRENDA. (*to ROBIN*)
WHY YOU LOOK A BIT DEPRESSED DEAR
  ROBIN. No, not at all.
  BRENDA.
THINGS GO BETTER WITH A SMILE

VALERIE.
I THINK SHE RUNS ON BATTERIES
BRENDA.
THIS YEAR
SANDRA-KAY. Hi, Mrs. Freelander.
BRENDA.
THIS IS GONNA BE A SWELL YEAR
SANDRA-KAY. Your hair looks great.
BRENDA. You like it? Thank you.
SO DOES YOURS, DEAR
SANDRA-KAY. Oh. Thanks alot.
BRENDA.
NOW, I'LL BE BACK IN JUST A . . .
ROBIN.
SEE MOM,
THINGS AREN'T WHAT I THOUGHT THEY'D BE MOM
THEY KEEP TELLING US IT'S NOT A COMPETITION
THEN THESE FEELINGS STRIKE,

FEELINGS I DON'T UNDERSTAND
AND I'M NOT SURE I LIKE . . .

DORIA. (*enters dressing rooms and finds ROBIN*) It's like a madhouse out there. You can't think. It's so intense, all the excitement. Rob, it's just insane.

ROBIN. I know just what you mean. I was telling Father Murphy how crazy it all . . .

DORIA. Murphy the judge? You got to a judge? For a talk? On your own?

ROBIN. It wasn't like that. He's got a sister in . . .

DORIA. Did you mention your Dad?

ROBIN. No.

DORIA. You're a fool. I'm telling you Rob . . . you can get orphan points.

ROBIN. I don't want them. (*DORIA kneels beside ROBIN. Lights focus on the two of them and dim on the other GIRLS.*)

DORIA. For an honor student, you're pretty dumb about beauty pageants. This one's in the bag if you . . .

ROBIN. In the bag? Doria, you're crazy.

DORIA. Am I? All my life I've waited for tonight. And now I know it won't be me . . . crowned and waving to the crowd. It won't be me. But maybe . . . maybe . . .
ROBIN, YOU'RE SPECIAL

ROBIN, YOU SPARKLE. LOOK THERE AND SEE
ROBIN IT'S TRUE
DO IT FOR ME
 Robin. I'm just a nervous wreck. I don't know if . . .
 Doria.
ROBIN, I KNOW HOW
ROBIN, I FEEL HOW STRONG YOU CAN BE
DON'T SAY YOU'RE NOT
GIVE IT A SHOT
DO IT FOR ME

HOME IN MY ROOM THERE'S A WALL FULL A
 PICTURES
BEAUTIFUL GIRLS, GIRLS WHO WIN
YOU'LL NEVER KNOW HOW I'VE LONGED TO BE
 ONE OF THEM, TOO
HOME IN MY ROOM THERE'S A DRAWER FULL
 OF CLIPPINGS,
CONTESTS I'LL NEVER BE IN,
MAGIC I WON'T BE A PART OF
EXCEPT THROUGH YOU

SO TURN TO THE MIRROR
LOOK AT THE PICTURE. TELL ME, WHO'S SHE?
ROBIN, YOU KNOW
ROBIN, YOU GLOW
ROBIN, PLEASE GO OUT THERE
AND DO IT FOR ME
 Carol. (*enters*) Girls—Your attention! Girls—Your
attention!
 Brenda.
ATTENTION GIRLS,
SO I CAN MAKE THIS SHORT AND SWEET
THERE'S SOMEONE HERE YOU'VE WAITED
ALL WEEK LONG TO MEET
HE'S ON THE RADIO; YOU'VE SEEN HIM ON T.V.
TED FARLEY FROM LOS ANGELES, THAT
 FABULOUS EMCEE

(*TED FARLEY enters. A leathery tan, rouge-rosy cheeks, and
 dyed hair give him the look of a waxworks figure. His game-
 show-host manner is unctuous and slightly daffy. He wears a
 sequined tuxedo jacket.*)

TED.
HI GIRLS,
NICE TO MEETCHA, DON'T BE SHY GIRLS
I'M AN ORDINARY GUY GIRLS
    DANA.
GET THE JACKET
    COOKIE.
GET THE HOOK
    PATTI-LYNN.
I HEARD HE KNOWS THE PRESIDENT
    TED.
TRUE GIRLS,
KNOW HIM WELL — AND NANCY TOO, GIRLS
LOOKIE WHAT I GOT FOR YOU GIRLS
COPIES OF MY LATEST BOOK

"JESUS WRITES MY PUNCHLINES"

LATER, WHEN THE SHOW IS THROUGH
CATCH ME AND I'LL AUTOGRAPH A COPY JUST
    FOR YOU
FULL OF FUN AND ANECDOTES
PLUS TONS OF INSPIRATION
IT'S TERRIFIC, READ THE QUOTES:
"A gem of Christian comedy" . . .
    BRENDA. Ted . . .
    TED. Jerry Falwell. "Heartwarming and hysterical" . . .
    BRENDA. Ted —
    TED. Pearl Bailey
"A Happy Trail to Hilarity" . . . Roy and Dale Rogers
    BRENDA.
THANK YOU TED, WE'RE GRATEFUL
YOU'RE SO THOUGHTFUL
    TED.
NOT A BIT.
    BRENDA.
BUT WE MUST DISMISS THE GIRLS NOW. IT'S
    HALF-HOUR . . .
    GIRLS. (*starting back for the dressing rooms*)
HOLY SHIT!

WHY'D I EVER COME UP HERE?
WHY DID I DO THIS?

(Light change. Set transition. We leave the dressing rooms and are now onstage, moments before the pageant is to begin. TONY passes by, pushing a slide projector. SHAWN approaches him.)

SHAWN. Are those the slides for the introductions?
TONY. Sure are.
SHAWN. That's so exciting! Can I see mine?
TONY. You're Miss . . .
SHAWN. La Jolla.
GIRLS.
PLEASE GOD, MAKE A MIRACLE
AND GET ME THROUGH THIS!

(BIG BOB enters, nearby. TONY sees him and moves toward him, leaving SHAWN alone near the projector. She's doing something with it. We can't make out quite what.)

TONY. Bob — say, Big Bob.
BIG BOB. Hey, Tony. Whatcha doin'?
TONY. Oh, they got me runnin' the slide projector. Say, Big Bob, me and the missus, we made our decision, we are gonna take it.
BIG BOB. The R.V.?
TONY. The red one.
BIG BOB. (*His other, "salesman" self appears.*) Well congratulations, son . . . and I'll tell ya what. I'm gonna have sports stripes professionally painted on the side of that sucker, no charge to you, because "Big Bob Freelander's Customers . . .
TONY. "Are also His Friends."

(SHAWN, by now, has completed whatever it was she was doing with the slide projector. TONY leaves BIG BOB, retrieves his projector, and pushes it offstage. Meanwhile, BRENDA enters and spots her husband. She's dressed to the nines.)

BRENDA. Bob — Are the judges ready?
BIG BOB. Sure are. And here's the envelope with the five finalists.
BRENDA. I'm dying to peek. But I won't.
BIG BOB. Brenda —
BRENDA. Yes?
BIG BOB. You look. So beautiful.

(*WORKMEN,   TOMMY,   CAROL,   WILSON-SHEARS,*
   GIRLS, and VOLUNTEERS swarm on in the last moments
   of preparation.)

ALL.
THIS YEAR
   CAROL.
IT'S SO EXCITING
   ALL.
THIS IS GONNA BE A SWELL YEAR
   LOUISE.
I LOVE THE LIGHTING
   WILSON-SHEARS.
VERY POLISHED, I CAN TELL, DEAR
   BRENDA.
WHY THANK YOU
   TOMMY. (*As WILSON-SHEARS parts the house curtain and*
pokes his head through:) What's he doing?
   WILSON-SHEARS.
JEEZ, YOU'VE GOT A CROWD!
   TOMMY.
TELL HIM THE HOUSE IS OPEN, PLEASE
   ALL.
THIS YEAR
   CAROL. These broke.
   TOMMY. Forget it.
   ALL.
THIS IS GONNA BE THE BEST YEAR
   WORKMAN. That's falling.
   TOMMY. Let it.
   ALL.
THIS IS GONNA BE FROM OVERTURE TO
   RECESSIONAL
COMPLETELY SLICK AND PROFESSIONAL
THIS YEAR, THIS YEAR, THIS . . .

(*TOMMY gestures. Everything stops and the GIRLS group*
   around him for the traditional pre-show pep-talk.)

   TOMMY. Ladies, in a few minutes you're going to be professional entertainers. Now, I know alot of you are scared and don't
think you can do it. But I've watched you all week and I know you
can. I'd like you to think about a seventeen year old kid who came

to me when I was staging an act for Sing Out, America! This girl hadn't had a lick of experience, but she wanted to try so bad, we just had to let her. That was eight years ago and today that girl is one of Sing Out, America's lead dancers. Now, that may not seem like much to you. But that girl, ladies, that girl had a wooden foot. (*The GIRLS stand stock-still for a moment, not quite sure what this means. After a beat they disperse, brows still knit. When they have cleared, TED FARLEY steps forward, clamps an arm around TOMMY, and confides seriously:*)

TED. That's a beautiful story, Tom. I'm always looking for inspirational youth stories for my radio show. May I use that one?

TOMMY. Be my guest. (*beat*) But it's total bullshit.

[MUSIC #15 *SMILE*]

(*TOMMY exits. Blackout. Fanfare.*)

VOICE. (*in black*) Good evening, ladies and gentlemen. And welcome to California's 1985 Young American Miss State Pageant. Hosted by California's very own Sunshine Boy . . . (*A spotlight finds him.*) Ted Farley.

(*TED holds an embarrassingly long time for applause that finally comes. A musical vamp begins, lights come up to reveal a sparkling curtain, and we are onstage. The pageant has begun.*)

TED. You know, they told me they wanted to get someone younger to do the pageant this year. But George Burns wasn't available. (*He fumbles with his cards.*) Bear with me. The girls are here. I've seen 'em. Here we are. Oh . . . I sing. I know this song, alright. We use it every year at the National Finals in Baton Rouge. I sing it. Not Bert Parks. They don't let him sing anything anymore. My camera, please. (*Someone hands him a camera.*) Here goes. (*He sings as pictures of GIRLS flash on screens around and above him.*)
HOLD THAT POSE
WANNA PICTURE OF EYES LIKE THOSE
WANNA CAPTURE THAT TURNED-UP NOSE
THAT REMARKABLE CHIN
HOLD THAT, PLEASE
FACE THE CAMERA AND SAY SWISS CHEESE

WATCH THE BIRDIE!
THAT'S GREAT! NOW FREEZE
THAT INCREDIBLE GRIN!

WHEN YOU'VE GOT TWO
DEEP DIMPLES
IT'S SINFUL NOT TO
HAVE 'EM PHOTOGRAPHED,
GRAB A SHOT TO
KNOCK 'EM FLAT IN THE AISLE.

SO HOLD REAL STILL
GIVE M'LITTLE OLD LENS A THRILL
FOCUS HERE AND M'CAMERA WILL
RECORD THAT
SMILE
I WANT THAT
SMILE
I LOVE THAT
SMILE
Yes, California! Here, tonight, the judges will choose your new
Young American Miss. And placing the crown on that lucky,
beautiful, and talented girl's head will be last year's winner. Let's
meet her now and wish her well in these last, golden moments of
her glorious reign. California's Young American Miss for 1984
—Joanne Marshall! (*Enter JOANNE. TED links arms to stroll
with her through a memory lane of her year in photographs,
flashing on screens.*)
WALK WITH ME
THROUGH THE HALLWAYS OF MEMORY
A PICTORIAL GALLERY
OF THIS MARVELOUS YEAR
COME AND SEE
EACH FLEETING INSTANT OF GLORY
FASHION SHOWS AND DINNERS
DONNY OSMOND MEETS THE WINNERS
COSTUME BALLS
AND OPENING SHOPPING MALLS
FILM RECALLS YOUR TRIUMPHS BRIGHT AND CLEAR
TRUE THEY DISAPPEAR
AH BUT NEVER FEAR, JOANNE
EVERY PRECIOUS MOMENT'S CAPTURED HERE

JOANNE. Thank you, Ted. Yes ladies and gentlemen tonight is
the last hour of my reign. But don't worry. There are sixteen of
this State's best and brightest High School about-to-be seniors,
waiting in the wings. It's a real privilege to introduce them to you.
This year's Young American Miss contestants.

(*Music builds. A curtain parts and there they are in a stage-set
resembling an antique valentine: all twenty-four GIRLS
wearing ice-cream parlor 'old-fashioned' finery. They carry
parasols.*)

GIRLS.
HOLD THAT POSE
TAKE A PICTURE

A SHOT THAT SHOWS
EVERY ONE OF US GLEAMS AND GLOWS
WITH A SPECIAL APPEAL

AIM RIGHT HERE
SNAP A SHOT TO MAKE
CRYSTAL CLEAR
FOR THE PERMANENT RECORD. WE'RE
LOOKIN SWELL AS WE FEEL

SHINE THAT LIGHT TO
ILLUMINATE
THIS, OUR NIGHT TO
GO FOR GOLDEN
IT'S ONLY RIGHT TO
LET IT LAST FOR A WHILE

SO HOLD REAL STILL
WHILE WE SAVOR THIS SPECIAL CHILL
AND THE MAN WITH THE CAMERA WILL
RECORD THAT
SMILE
C'MON, KID
SMILE
OKAY, KID
SMILE

(*ORCH. GIRLS do a choreographed parasol dance. As part of the choreography, each GIRL has a moment to stand in the spotlight and open her parsol in time to the music.*)

LINDA. I'm smiling because my costume by Laguna Sport was designed and manufactured right here in the State of California.

DEBRALEE. I'm smiling because last year, California citrus fruits out-sold Florida citrus fruits, three to one!

HEIDI. I'm smiling because the Oakland A's are on their way to a pennant! Go guys!

(*The parasol dance continues. But when ROBIN's moment comes to stand in the spotlight and open her parasol, it doesn't work. The parasol jams, then breaks completely. She's mortified, completely thrown. She freezes, looks at the audience in terror and runs offstage, into the wings. TOMMY FRENCH catches her there and blocks her exit:*)

TOMMY. Hey, hey, hey. Where do you think you're going?

ROBIN. (*wildly*) It broke! I didn't know what to do! I'm so embarrassed, I . . .

CONNIE-SUE. (*Onstage*) I'm smiling because our governor is really doing something about earthquake control.

GIRLS.
WHEN YOU'VE GOT TWO
DEEP DIMPLES
IT'S SINFUL NOT TO
HAVE 'EM PHOTOGRAPHED,
GRAB A SHOT TO
KNOCK 'EM FLAT IN THE AISLE.

(*Back to ROBIN and TOMMY in the wings:*)

TOMMY. Look, you just had a lucky break.

ROBIN. I did?

TOMMY. Sure. They noticed you. There are girls'd pray for that to happen. Now go out there and use it! (*ROBIN nervously makes her way back onstage, where the number is still in progress.*)

TED.
SO HOLD REAL STILL

GIVE M'LITTLE OLD LENS A THRILL
FOCUS HERE AND M'CAMERA WILL
RECORD THAT
SMILE

(*TED holds out a microphone. Several GIRLS line up for their turn to speak into it. This is part of the choreography. ROBIN is last in this line.*)

PATTI-LYNN. Cause there's still a Californian in the Whitehouse!
GIRLS.
SMILE!
DANA. Cause they're rebuilding the Pacific Coast Highway!
GIRLS.
SMILE!
GINA. Cause Knott's Berry Farm has the world's fastest rollercoaster!
GIRLS.
SMILE!
MARIA. Cause our citizens have equal opportunity!
GIRLS.
SMILE!
ROBIN. (*ad-libbing*) Cause even if your umbrella breaks, who needs an umbrella when it's summertime in Southern California?
TOMMY. (*in the wings*) They learn fast.

(*The number is ready for its Big Finish and here's how it goes: One by one, each GIRL gets a moment to dance Center into a spotlight, as an enormous photograph of her smiling face is projected onto the backdrop. It's a sort of "Parade of States" effect. As part of the choreography, each GIRL is required to spin upstage and pose, facing her picture, arms wide.*)

GIRLS.
HOLD THAT POSE
(*Picture #1*)
WANNA PICTURE OF EYES LIKE THOSE
(*Picture #2*)
WANNA CAPTURE THAT TURNED-UP NOSE
(*Picture #3*)

THAT REMARKABLE CHIN . . .
   TED. Let's hear it, folks. Aren't they something?
   GIRLS.
HOLD THAT, PLEASE
(*Picture #4*)
FACE THE CAMERA AND SAY SWISS CHEESE
(*Picture #5*)
WATCH THE BIRDIE!
THAT'S GREAT! NOW FREEZE
(*Picture #6*)
THAT INCREDIBLE GRIN!
   TED & GIRLS.
SOMEDAY WHEN YOU
(*Picture #7*)
GET OLDER
YOU'LL FEEL A YEN TO
(*Picture #8*)
PULL THE ALBUM OUT
THANK ME THEN YOU
(*Picture #9*)
PUT THIS MOMENT ON FILE
   GIRLS.
GET OUR MOMENT ON FILE

SO HOLD THAT POSE
(*Picture #10*)
AND IF EVER A COLD WIND BLOWS
(*Picture #11*)
YOU CAN TURN TO YOUR LONG AGOS
(*Picture #12*)
TO FIND THAT
SMILE
(*Picture #13*)
C'MON KID,
SMILE
(*Picture #14*)
OKAY, KID
SMILE
I WANT THAT
I NEED THAT

(*Picture #15: MARIA GONZALES. This is the last photograph.*

*But instead of her smiling portrait, MARIA's photo shows her
stark naked against the white tiles of the shower-room upstairs. When she turns upstage to face the picture, it's as if she
has been shot. She freezes as the other girls scoot into position
around her to finish the number.)*

I LOVE THAT
SMILE!!

[MUSIC #15A *SMILE PLAYOFF*]

*(Light change. Set transition. The pageant revolves upstage and
away from us, as our attention turns to the backstage area.
The adult volunteers are in shock at what has just happened.
First MARIA GONZALES and then the other GIRLS come
running backstage. Onstage, TED plows on as if nothing had
happened:)*

TED. A beautiful batch of girls, aren't they, ladies and gentlemen? I think they get prettier and prettier every year. But you
know, folks as glowingly beautiful as these kids are, the judges
here tonight are looking at a whole lot more than physical beauty.

MARIA. (*In Spanish, backstage:*) Alright, who did it! I wanna
know, who did it? I wanna know. I wanna . . . (*She bursts into
tears. LOUISE holds her as BRENDA enters.*)

BRENDA. (*shooing the GIRLS who are lingering in the wings*)
Alright girls, things can't stop. Things can't stop. You've got an
audience out there. Fifteen hundred people. Get into your next
costumes. Carry on as usual. Get moving. (*The GIRLS do as
they're told and exit. BRENDA turns her attention to MARIA,
who is still sobbing in CAROL's arms.*) Maria—you've got to
pull yourself together dear. You've got to perform your talent
act . . .

MARIA. You don't expect me to go back out there!

BRENDA. You've got to.

MARIA. You're crazy. All those people looking at me like
that . . .

TED. (*from onstage*) Now as many of you know, last evening
the girls competed in individual categories . . .

BRENDA. Maria . . . I'm sure there isn't anyone here who
blames you for what happened.

TED. We'd like to present to you now, the winner of last night's
talent award—

BRENDA. I want you to show your courage and perseverance . . .

TED. Performing the act for which she won our Performing Arts Scholarship . . .

BRENDA. Just go out there just like nothing happened.

TED. Salinas' Young American Miss . . .

MARIA. But something did happen.

TED. Maria Gonzales!

MARIA. One of them did it. One of your girls.

TED. Maria Gonzales!

MARIA. And we both know why. (*She exits quickly.*)

BRENDA. (*in a panic*) Maria! Maria, come back here and . . .

CAROL. Forget it, Brenda. She's gone.

BRENDA. Oh my God, Carol, what'll I do? Are the Pom-Pom Girls ready yet?

CAROL. Well, they've started but . . .

BRENDA. Hurry them up! Tony, what's he doing out there?

TONY. I don't know. Just sort of . . . talking.

TED. And that girl, ladies and gentlemen, that girl had a wooden foot.

BRENDA. Oh, God! Get the girls!

[MUSIC #16 *GET THE GIRLS*]

(*GIRLS with Pom-Poms go onstage and start performing. Meanwhile, we focus on several other GIRLS who are backstage, getting ready to go on:*)

PERFORMING GIRLS.
LOOK AT ME!
I'M A YOUNG AMERICAN MISS!

KIMBERLY. It had to be an inside job. It looked like it was taken in the shower room.

SHAWN. It was probably some pervert's idea of a joke.

VALERIE. Well it was someone's idea of a joke.

ROBIN. God, Doria. It's getting so weird.

DORIA. Don't even think about it.

ROBIN. But do you know what crossed my mind when they flashed that awful picture? The one, first thing I thought? Before I felt sorry for her? Before anything? Do you know what I felt?

DORIA. Yeah. You felt thank God it wasn't you and that's one less in competition. I know. We all felt it. Every girl here.

BRENDA. (*enters*) Hurry girls! The Pom-Pom cue!

(*At BRENDA's urging, the GIRLS join the Pom-Pom routine onstage. As they move, WILSON-SHEARS comes bombing in backstage, extremely agitated.*)

WILSON-SHEARS. Mrs. Freelander. It's a catastrophe out front. No-one's paying attention. No-one's listening. They're all talking about that . . . that . . .

BRENDA. (*beside herself, sure the job is lost*) Mr. Wilson-Shears, we're so sorry. We don't know how it could have happened but . . .

WILSON-SHEARS. You know the Foundation could sue that Mexican girl for pulling a stunt like that. I don't want her back onstage, do you hear me?

BRENDA. I . . . I sent her home.

WILSON-SHEARS. It's a disaster out there. They're whispering. Some of them were even laughing right out loud at the scholarship film.

BRENDA. (*to herself, miserably*) Laughing. Oh my God.

WILSON-SHEARS. It's a nightmare. A nightmare.

BRENDA. (*An idea strikes her.*) No. No. Not if I can help it. (*She springs into action.*) Carol — Tell the girls I'll announce the next part. Just listen for the cue. (*She starts madly rummaging through papers.*) The envelope, where's the envelope?

WILSON-SHEARS. What are you talking about? What are you . . .

BRENDA. She won Talent last night and they voted before . . . (*ripping open the envelope and crossing something off of the card*) Just as I thought. (*standing erect and starting toward the stage*) Carol, give me your corsage.

WILSON-SHEARS. Mrs. Freelander, may I ask what you're going?

BRENDA. I've worked too long, Mr. Wilson-Shears. Much too long and much too hard to . . . excuse me. (*She moves toward the stage.*)

WILSON-SHEARS. Mrs. Freelander . . . What's she up to?

CAROL. I don't know.

(*Light change. Set transition. The pageant revolves to face us. In the wings, SHEARS, CAROL, and others anxiously watch to see what BRENDA is up to. Our attention is focused off the*

backstage area now and onto the pageant itself, where the
GIRLS are just finishing their Pom-Pom routine:)

GIRLS.
GO AND TELL UNCLE SAM
THAT HIS NIECE IS A Y.A.M.!
SHE'S A YOUNG AMERICAN MISS!
    TED. Aren't they something, Ladies and Gentlemen? Let's give
them a . . . (*BRENDA marches herself onstage and approaches
the startled TED. The GIRLS just stand there, having no idea
what's going on.*)
    BRENDA. Excuse me . . . Ted . . . thank you. (*TED, con-
fused, moves to one side. BRENDA faces the audience and speaks
with a charming nervousness.*) Ladies and gentlemen. My goodness, there are so many of you. Ladies and gentlemen, I'm Brenda
DiCarlo Freelander, Jaycette Coordinator of this year's pageant
and I'm not much used to speaking in public. But something has
happened here tonight. Something which requires me to speak
and to speak now. Moments ago, on this very stage, a cruel joke
was played. A cynical and smutty trick whose vicious aim was
unmistakably to tear down the Young American Miss Experience. To humiliate it. To make it appear foolish. Foolish. (*She
looks out at the house, sees that they're listening attentively, and
eases into her pitch:*) Now I know many of you. From
church . . . Jaycees . . . from P.T.A. And many of you know
me, but I wonder how many of you remember a night, 'many
years ago, when on this very runway I was crowned your Young
American Miss. When I received a scholarship that helped me get
through Santa Rosa Junior College. When I received that pre-
paid airline pass to Baton Rouge where I would make so many
friends . . . and memories. Well, I have devoted myself ever
since to seeing that each year another girl receives that self-same
Golden Opportunity. And I ask you Santa Rosa. Is that foolish?
Does that seem a fitting target for derision? Don't the marvelous
young ladies waiting in the wings right now deserve the same
Bright-Shining Chance I had? (*She's on a roll now and she knows
it. There's a little Eva Peron in her as she continues in an impas-
sioned, oratorical vein:*) If you feel with me the answer is Of-
Course-They-Do. If you believe with me this pageant represents
the Best Hopes of our nation's youth, I ask you to forget the act of
vandalism we have seen performed tonight and turn your
thoughts instead to what is right about our youth, about America,

and applaud them with me, won't you? Oh, if you believe, please clap your hands. Yes, put your hands together and applaud this year's Young American Miss contestants as we joyfully announce the names of this year's lovely finalists, [MUSIC #16A *THE FINALISTS*] (*During the preceding, without missing a beat, she has cued the band for a fanfare.*) And Ted . . . I have the envelope—Here! (*She now returns the microphone to TED, who takes it and tries to keep the ball in the air.*)

TED. Thank you Mrs. Freelander. And now, in this envelope I have the names of the five girls . . .

BRENDA. Ted . . . (*holds up her fingers*)

TED. Excuse me, four girls, whom the judges have selected as this year's finalists. And now . . . as the big moment approaches . . . how ya feelin' girls? Ya nervous? Yeah, me too. Okay . . . The five . . . four . . . finalists in this year's California Young American Miss Pageant . . . in no particular order . . . Shawn Christianson . . . Sandra Kay MacAffee . . . Robin Gibson . . . and Doria Hudson! There they are folks! Let's get a good look at them and learn a little more about them in depth!

[MUSIC #17 *WE WISH WE WERE YOU*]

THE ELEVEN NON-FINALISTS. (*Onstage*)
WE WISH WE WERE YOU
YOU, FABULOUS, FAN-TABULOUS YOU!
YOU, YOU'RE THE PERFECT COMBINATION!
YOU, YOU'RE A SOURCE OF INSPIRATION!

(*One by one, each finalist steps forward to smile and wave as TED reads a blurb about her. As this is proceeding, however, a light and set transition begins. The pageant revolves away from us and our focus returns to the backstage area.*)

TED. (*Onstage*) A Junior at Antelope Valley High, Robin's hobbies are biking, creative writing and music—classical to rock. This year's Scholastic Achievement winner, Robin enjoys handicrafts, gourmet cooking, and remembers friends on holidays by making her own greeting cards.

GIRLS.
WE WISH WE WERE YOU!

(*By now the transition is complete and we're in the wings. On one side, BRENDA is receiving accolades. On the other, ROBIN comes offstage, stunned.*)

CAROL. Oh, Brenda, that was so beautiful. I'm sure they've forgotten about the other thing completely by now.

TONY. That was swell. Just swell!

BRENDA. Thank you. Thank you. (*She exits.*)

TED. (*Onstage, during the above:*) Hailing from beautiful Yuba City, Doria Hudson organized her school's Jazzercize Club. Some of her favorite things include long walks on the beach, Garfield the cat, and Mrs. Field's Coconut/Macadamia cookies.

GIRLS.
WE WISH WE WERE YOU . . .

TED. A native of La Jolla . . . Shawn's hobbies are . . .

DORIA. (*Coming offstage and joining ROBIN:*) I don't believe it I don't believe it I don't believe it I don't be . . .

ROBIN. I told you.

DORIA. But I didn't win an O.A. This is like really rare for—Oh my God, I haven't written a "What It Means To Me." I wasn't expecting . . . Maybe I should do God, but I don't know. Sandra-Kay's probably gonna do that. She's born-again or something. Robin, did I lose a lash? I think I lost a . . .

ROBIN. You're fine. Hey, we're competing again, aren't we?

DORIA. Hm? Oh. Yeah. Yeah, I guess we are. Good luck.

ROBIN. You too.

GIRLS.
WE WISH WE WERE YOU . . .

(*They go back onstage, as do the other Finalists. As the following scene plays, the music underscoring the 'onstage' number will tail down, leaving the girls dancing, their backs to us, first with sketchy accompaniment, and then in silence. This is a dramatic effect that leaves us focused on the action backstage, the pageant serving only as background.*)

BRENDA. (*sailing back in like a cyclone*) Tony—Go through every one of the finale slides and make sure nothing else has been tampered with. Oh, do I need a Pepsi.

BIG BOB. I'll get you one, honey.

BRENDA. Bob . . . Oh, Bob. Was I alright?

BIG BOB. You were great. You're soaking wet too. I don't think I've ever seen you nervous before.

BRENDA. Well all those people, Bob . . .

BIG BOB. Honey, can we go into the office and talk?

BRENDA. I can't take the time now. How are the judges? What did Father Murphy say?

BIG BOB. It's the judges we've got to talk about, Brenda. It's serious. (*beat*) They don't think we ought to pick a winner.

BRENDA. What are you talking about?

BIG BOB. Look, for all we know one of the girls sneaked that picture and planted it. Tony says it's the only way it could've happened. For all we know we'd be picking the girl who did it. Not to mention that one of the girls was unfairly disqualified and . . .

BRENDA. They can't do this.

BIG BOB. It's how they feel. That was a beautiful speech you made, Bren. And if you believe it . . . about how the pageant does mean something and is important, we'll declare this one invalid, investigate, and start again.

BRENDA. This can't be happening. Robert, you're head judge. You're Dean of Judges. Talk to the others. Convince them. They've got to pick a winner.

BIG BOB. You don't understand, honey. I know I'm head judge. I'm the one who's telling them they can't.

BRENDA. You? (*beat*) Why are you doing this to me?

BIG BOB. Not to you. Brenda, I love you. But I don't understand what's been going on here this week.

BRENDA. We're getting things on. We're getting things done.

BIG BOB. No matter what? No matter who falls off the platform? No matter who gets hurt and embarrassed? No matter who wins?

BRENDA. You're making mountains out of . . .

BIG BOB. I don't think so.

BRENDA. I'm getting tired of you preaching at me, Robert. Are you so perfect? Is everything at your precious motor world so perfect? Is every discount what it says it is? Can all your customers really afford . . .

BIG BOB. That's business. This is supposed to be different.

BRENDA. Well, maybe it's not. But it's my business. I'm the pageant coordinator. I pick the judges. And . . . And if you want to resign . . . right now . . . I'll accept your resignation.

You don't have to pick a winner, Bob. But believe me I will see that someone does.

(She exits. The GIRLS on the pageant stage exit too. Music begins. BIG BOB slowly crosses downstage, troubled. On the pageant stage, ROBIN enters holding a candle and wearing a white gown. She sings:)

[MUSIC #18 *IN OUR HANDS*]

ROBIN.
TO EVERY THING THERE IS A SEASON, WE KNOW
A TIME TO KEEP AND THEN A TIME TO LET GO . . .

(Set and light transition. The pageant stage changes position and starts to drift upstage, away from us. BIG BOB crosses downstage, where lights pick out a bench and a few bushes. Moonlight. For the first time this evening, we are "outside the building". BOB stands there in the shadows, lost in thought. Upstage, we can still see and hear the pageant.)

ROBIN (*continued*).
TURN AROUND AND LIFT YOUR EYES
YOUR CHILDREN RISE WITH DREAMS TO SPIN

(A procession of GIRLS appears, joining ROBIN. They are in white, holding candles)

GIRLS.
YOU'VE RAISED THEM TALL YOU'VE TAUGHT
    THEM WELL,
NOW TIME MUST TELL, AS THEY BEGIN

WE ARE YOUR OWN, WE ARE YOUR CHILDREN
WE ARE THE FUTURE THAT YOU'VE MADE
WE FACE THE WORLD YOU SET BEFORE US
UNAFRAID . . .

(Not far from him, BIG BOB hears a rustling in the bushes. He quietly moves toward it. Lights reveal the people hidden in the bushes: LITTLE BOB and FREDDY. They aren't aware of BOB's presence. But he hears them.)

LITTLE BOB. I gotta hand it to ya, Freddy. These pictures are incredible.

FREDDY. Yeah, but I didn't know they were gonna end up onstage.

LITTLE BOB. Look, it's great advertising. Now these are full frontals for Gary. Fifteen apiece. He owes us thirty bucks. And tell him I'll throw in this one.

FREDDY. Jeez!

LITTLE BOB. At only five bucks extra because Little Bob Freelander's Customers . . .

BOTH. Are also his friends.

(FREDDY exits. BIG BOB steps back into the shadows as LITTLE BOB looks around furtively and then exits, counting money. Upstage at the pageant, each of the Finalists now has a chance to step forward with her candle and speak:)

GIRLS.
IN OUR HANDS
SANDRA-KAY. (*stepping forward*) As Young American Miss . . .
GIRLS.
WE TAKE THIS WORLD
SANDRA-KAY. I'd like to set an example for young women everywhere.
GIRLS.
AND IN OUR HANDS THIS WORLD IS NEW
SHAWN. As Young American Miss, I'd like to share my talents with others.
GIRLS.
IN OUR HANDS
DORIA. As Young American Miss
GIRLS.
YOU PLACE THE DREAM
DORIA. I'd like to reach out to people around the world.
GIRLS.
WITH OUR HANDS WE WORK IT THROUGH

(Outside, BIG BOB sees MARIA GONZALES, leaving the building, carrying a suitcase. He watches as she sadly moves offstage, going home.)

GIRLS.
WE ARE YOUR OWN, WE ARE YOUR CHILDREN
YOU'VE WATCHED US GROW AS CHILDREN MUST
NOW ALL WE ASK IS FOR YOUR BLESSING
AND YOUR TRUST . . .
YOUR TRUST . . .
AS IN OUR HANDS

(*MARIA is gone now. Upstage, ROBIN steps forward.*)

ROBIN. As Young American Miss . . .
GIRLS.
WE TAKE THIS EARTH
ROBIN. I'd like to make my father proud of me.
GIRLS.
TO MAKE THIS EARTH OUR OWN
ROBIN. He passed away when I was two years old.
GIRLS.
RELEASE OUR HANDS, WATCH US STAND ALONE

(*TOMMY FRENCH comes outside, carrying his suitcase. He sees BIG BOB sitting on the bench and notices that something seems to be wrong. He goes to him.*)

TOMMY. Hey, what're you doin' out here? I thought you judge-types were inside deliberating.
BIG BOB. You're leaving?
TOMMY. Thought I'd avoid the crowd.
BIG BOB. You did a swell job.
TOMMY. Yeah. Took a nice bunch of high school kids, and turned 'em into Vegas showgirls. I would like to know who the hell took that picture, though.
BIG BOB. It was my son.
TOMMY. (*softly, after a beat*) Wow.
BIG BOB. (*A silence, then he changes the subject.*) You've, uh, got your check?
TOMMY. Your wife gave it to me. Minus the deduction. That was one hell of a speech she made. She'd probably make a politician.
BIG BOB. Probably.
TOMMY. But do me and the country a favor, will ya? Keep her

in beauty pageants. (*beat*) Hey look, I know you tried about the ramp. I've got eyes and I appreciate it. C'mon, cheer up. A drop more optimism, a drop more energy, a drop more perseverance. That's what you're supposed to have isn't it?

BIG BOB. Me?

TOMMY. Sure. It's obvious, Mr. Freelander. There's only one real Young American Miss around here . . . and it's you. (*beat*) Til next year, huh?

(*TOMMY exits. As the number concludes, there is a set and light transition. The pageant stage rolls toward us, carrying the singing GIRLS. BIG BOB exits and the "outdoors" disappear. By the song's emotional final chords, our focus has completely returned to the pageant, which fills the entire stage:*)

GIRLS.
SO IN OUR HANDS

WE TAKE THIS EARTH

OTHER GIRLS.
OUR HANDS CAN HELP, THEY CAN HOLD
OUR HANDS CAN SHAPE, THEY CAN MOLD

ALL.
TO MAKE THIS EARTH OUR OWN
AND YES, WE ARE YOUR CHILDREN
BE PROUD HOW WELL WE'VE GROWN
NOW TURN AROUND, LIFT YOUR EYES, WATCH US STAND
ALONE

(*TED and JOANNE enter downstage of the assembled girls. Drumroll.*)

TED. Joanne—I think I see something in your hands.

[MUSIC #18A *THE WINNER*]

JOANNE. Yes Ted. The judges have reached their decision.

TED. Then may I have the first envelope, please?

JOANNE. Here it is, Ted.

TED. Thank you, Joanne. (*He makes a big fuss about opening it.*) You know, either they put special glue on these things or . . .

JOANNE. I think it's the excitement, Ted.

TED. Yes it certainly is exciting, Joanne . . . and . . . (*He has it open.*) Here we are. Here, ladies and gentlemen, we are. And the First runner up . . . the young lady to assume the obligations of California's Young American Miss should she for any reason be unable to perform the duties of her crown. First Runner Up . . . From Beautiful Yuba City . . . An about-to-be senior at Mountainridge High . . . Doria Hudson! (*A spot hits DORIA. The look on her face is more than the expected joy and surprise of a beauty pageant winner. Before the smile breaks, she's in a complete and serious state of shock. Slowly, the smile grows as ROBIN grabs her hand from the other end of the line and urges her forward. Finally, DORIA's "professional" face emerges and she moves forward to accept a bouquet of roses from JOANNE.*) Congratulations, dear.

DORIA. Thank you . . . thank you . . .

TED. And Joanne, if I may please have the second envelope, please

JOANNE. Here it is, Ted.

TED. This is the one, California. The Girl to Beat at this year's Nationally Broadcast Nationwide Finals in Baton Rouge, Louisiana. California's Young American Miss for 1985. From Bakersfield, California, Home of California White Chablis . . . Sandra-Kay MacAffee!

[MUSIC #19 *THERE GOES THE GIRL*]

(*The others gather around Sandra-Kay in the usual hoopla. We have a moment, however, to catch ROBIN realizing that it's over and that the outcome is exactly as she herself would have predicted it a week ago. TED, meanwhile, continues:*) And before our eyes, ladies and gentlemen, the Old gives way to the new as Joanne Marshall places her crown on the shining head of California's Young American Miss . . . Sandra-Kay . . . MacAffee. Let's get a good look at her, as she walks in beauty and in triumph! (*And the runway walk begins — all popping flashbulbs, tears, waving, and smiles — as SANDRA-KAY walks and TED sings:*)

TED.

THERE GOES THE GIRL
AND IT SUDDENLY SEEMS SHE WAS BORN TO BE
FLOATING LIKE THIS
DOWN A RUNWAY OF GLIST'NING DREAMS

LOOK! ON HER CHEEK!
IT'S A DEAR SWEET TEAR OF HAPPINESS
AS SHE'S PARADING THE RADIANCE
THAT BROUGHT THIS HONOR DOWN UPON HER . . .

(*The pageant stage revolves to face away from us. Only TED and SANDRA-KAY remain on it. Meanwhile, our focus returns backstage, where the fifteen GIRLS break out of their pageant demeanor and start babbling, crying, squealing, and consoling each other. 'Onstage,' TED continues:*)

TED.
THERE GOES THE GIRL,
TELL ME WHAT IS SHE THINKING RIGHT NOW AS SHE
JOINS THE FORTUNATE FEW
EVERY GLANCE REVEALS
THE MOONSTRUCK MAGIC THAT SHE FEELS
THE WONDER OF WINNING
WHEN LIFE IS BEGINNING
AND YOUNG AMERICAN DREAMS COME TRUE!

DORIA. (*Spotting ROBIN off by herself, she breaks out of the crowd and goes to her.*) Robin! Rob! (*ROBIN hugs her hard.*) You know I actually wanted you to win too. I really did.

ROBIN. I know.

DORIA. Are you okay?

ROBIN. (*She isn't, but she covers and smiles.*) Oh . . . yeah. Yeah, I'm fine. (*An enormous squeal from the other girls announces SANDRA-KAY's arrival backstage.*)

TED. From all of us here at the Young American Miss Pageant . . . more heartfelt thanks to you . . . the Americans who make it all possible.

DORIA. How's my hair? They'll want me for pictures. Me. Pictures.

TED. And so, until next year at pageant time. Goodnight! God Bless! Think Young! And drive home safely! (*Upstage, a scrim descends and the pageant is officially over. Backstage, there is a lot of commotion. Pictures are being taken of SANDRA-KAY. DORIA stands nearby waiting to be asked for a picture.*)

BRENDA. Girls, girls, stand back please, won't you? We need a few shots of Sandra-Kay. Dave, here she is. Girls, you're free to change now. Parents and friends are being asked to wait in the Luther Burbank lounge. (*She notices DORIA standing there awkwardly.*) Congratulations, Doria.

DORIA. Thanks.

BRENDA. You'd better get started upstairs, dear. We've got to clear this stage. (*DORIA, realizing she's not going to be asked, looks at SANDRA-KAY then exits. BRENDA, continuing her organizational tour-de-force, doesn't notice WILSON-SHEARS enter and stand beaming at her with almost paternal pride.*) Dave — I'll need some with her town sash and some on the steps outside . . . (*She turns to see WILSON-SHEARS.*)

WILSON-SHEARS. You turned it around, for us. I'm very grateful.

BRENDA. I didn't do anything, sir.

WILSON-SHEARS. Oh yes you did, and there aren't many women who could have. Look, I'm getting a very early start tomorrow but I wonder — could you spare a moment tonight to meet me and several other of the pageant officials in our suite at the Ramada? I'd like them to meet you and there are a few things happening on the National level I'd like to tell you about . . . sound you out on.

BRENDA. (*answering The-Words-She's-Been-Waiting-to-Hear with The-Words-She's-Been-Waiting-to-Say:*) Mr. Wilson-Shears, I guess you know how much I love the work we do.

WILSON-SHEARS. Then you'll meet us in half an hour?

BRENDA. Perfect. (*SHEARS exits. BRENDA, who feels as if she'd just won the pageant herself, stands and savors her moment of triumph. Upstage, CAROL clears the stage.*)

CAROL. Okay Dave, let's get her out to the steps now . . . Everybody clear the stage. Tony . . . Louise . . . they've got to fly things out and . . .

(*Alone onstage now, BRENDA notices SANDRA-KAY's roses, lying on the floor, forgotten. She picks them up tenderly and stands for a moment holding them, remembering. She doesn't see BIG BOB enter silently, far upstage. He watches his wife for a long moment before speaking.*)

BIG BOB. You ready to go?

BRENDA. Oh . . . Bob you scared me. Sandra-Kay forgot her roses. I'll see that Carol gets them to her. She'll want to press them.

BIG BOB. Like we pressed yours.

BRENDA. Yes. Oh Bob, I'm so sorry about before. What with all that tension and crisis, I don't even know what I said.

BIG BOB. Let's not talk about it now.

BRENDA. No, let's not. Did you see the end? I voted, I think I voted the way you would've . . . Mr. Wilson-Shears thought it went well. He . . . uh . . . asked me to meet him at the suite for just a minute on our way home and . . . You're still mad at me, aren't you?

BIG BOB. I'm just tired.

BRENDA. Well I've got an idea, then. Why don't we check in at the Ramada tonight like you've wanted to all week? Hm? Why not? We deserve a treat. You know, I think I could relax tonight and . . .

BIG BOB. I think I'd just like to go home now.

BRENDA. Oh . . . Well you're probably right. Tell you what. I'll walk over to the Ramada now, talk to Shears and you'll meet me there with the car in half an hour. (*She starts out, then turns.*) You know, Bob, I don't think that picture spoiled anything. [MUSIC #20 *FINALE*] Not really. Not at all. I think we made it everything it's supposed to be. Everything. The best year. The best. (*She exits. BIG BOB is alone onstage. After a moment he begins to sing very softly:*)

BIG BOB.
TOMORROW I KNOW WE'LL DISCUSS IT,
FIGURE OUT HOW TO TALK TO THE KID,
WE'LL SIT DOWN AND DISCUSS
HOW THIS HAPPENED TO US,
AND TO HIM . . .
WHAT WE SAID . . .
WHAT HE DID

THEN WE'LL TELL OURSELVES EVERYTHING'S
   BETTER
THAT WE'VE TALKED IT ALL THROUGH, GOT IT
   RIGHT
AND BY MONDAY I'LL BET WE'LL COMPLETELY
   FORGET
WHAT WENT WRONG HERE TONIGHT
(*A beat, then quietly:*) What went wrong here tonight?

(*Upstage, we see GIRLS with suitcases, dress bags, makeup kits, on their way back to dressing rooms and dorms:*)

GIRLS.
TOMORROW THINGS GET BACK TO NORMAL

BIG BOB.
WE'LL SMILE AND PRETEND NOTHING HAPPENED
  GIRLS.
TOMORROW I GUESS LIFE GOES ON . . .
  BIG BOB.
WE'LL PICK OURSELVES UP AND GO ON . . .
  GIRLS.
WHERE'D THE CHEERING GO?
WHERE'D THE CHANCES GO?

IT'S SO STRANGE
HOW SO QUICK
IT'S ALL OVER
ALL GONE . . .
IT'S ALL GONE . . .
  BIG BOB.
IF THE PAGEANT COULD FEEL LIKE THE OLD DAYS
OH . . . WE'D LIKE THAT . . . WE'D LIKE THAT
  ALOT.
WE DON'T WANT IT TO END, SO WE'LL SAY LET'S
  PRETEND
LET'S GET ON WITH THE SHOW!
LET IT RIDE, LET IT GO!
LET'S FORGET WHAT WE . . .
No. No let's not.

*(BIG BOB turns and exits. ROBIN, lost in her own thoughts,
  appears among the GIRLS.)*

  GIRLS.
JUST A TYPICAL HIGH SCHOOL SENIOR . . .
  ROBIN.
ANTELOPE VALLEY YOUR YOUNG AMERICAN MISS
IS COMIN' HOME
SHE WON'T HAVE THE CROWN OR THE SASH OR
  THE GOWN
OR THE ROSES
SHE WON'T BE IN THE PAPERS
SHE WON'T BE ON T.V.
'FACT IT ISN'T REAL CLEAR
AS OF NOW,
AS OF HERE
WHAT SHE WILL TURN OUT TO BE . . .

(*ROBIN joins DORIA in their dorm room. ROBIN begins to change out of her gown. DORIA puts her bouquet on the bed, sets her crown on the dresser and starts brushing her hair.*)

DORIA. Think about it, Rob. Come with me. You've got a real shot at Miss Sunbelt. We both do.

ROBIN. Forget it, Doria.

DORIA. But we're a team now. I was so proud of you out there.

ROBIN. You really were, weren't you?

DORIA. It's like throwing a baby into a pool. They swim whether they want to or not. I'm tellin' you this Miss Sunbelt contest is too good to pass up. I've got all the brochures right here. No state residency requirements. Just a talent competition and bathing suits . . . (*DORIA exits into the bathroom, still babbling. ROBIN continues to pack and sing her thoughts.*)

ANTELOPE VALLEY YOUR YOUNG AMERICAN MISS
IS COMIN' HOME
IN FRONT OF THE CROWD, IT GOT WEIRD
SHE'S NOT PROUD OF WHAT HAPPENED
BUT NOW THAT'S ALL BEHIND HER
AND WHEN IT'S SAID AND DONE—
SHE'S NOT SORRY SHE LOST—
CAUSE IT FEELS, FUNNY THING,
IN SOME STRANGE WAY—
SHE WON!

AND ANTELOPE VALLEY YOUR YOUNG AMERICAN
   MISS
IS COMIN' HOME
TO BE WHO SHE CHOOSES TO BE
NOT WHAT ANYONE TELLS HER—
NO QUEEN OR PRINCESS
NO CROWN, NO PRIZE, NO THRONE.
YOUR AMERICAN MISS
WANTS ALOT MORE THAN THIS
SHE'S NOT SURE WHAT IT IS . . .
BUT SHE'LL FIND WHAT IT IS . . .
FOR HERSELF
AND ON HER . . .

DANA. (*coming to the door of the dressing room*) Robin . . . there's somebody outside for you. (*ROBIN looks out to see a middle-aged woman who has just entered upstage. She lights up.*)

ROBIN. Mom?! (*ROBIN's MOTHER nods and holds out her arms. ROBIN rushes to her. They hold in an embrace as DORIA re-enters, now wearing cut-offs and a sweatshirt.*)

DORIA. So whatdya say, Robin? Robin? Rob? (*DORIA turns to see ROBIN in her mother's arms. She's alone, very still, about to cry. A long moment. Then she turns and her eyes light upon the runner-up crown, sitting on the dressing table.*)

OFFSTAGE VOICES.

DISNEYLAND

MAGIC KINGDOM

DISNEYLAND

(*DORIA moves to the crown, touches it gently, then lifts it . . . And places it on her head.*)

SOMEONE GIVE ME DISNEYLAND . . .

(*She picks up her bouquet of roses and holds them. The pose of the winner.*)

TAKE ME THERE TO DISNEYLAND . . .

(*She's living the fantasy now—blocking out her loneliness with the dream. Lights change and the dorms seem a million miles away. DORIA is floating on a runway that hangs magically in space, twinkling like the stars among which it's suspended.*)

AND WHEN I GET TO DISNEYLAND . . .

(*DORIA raises an arm to wave to a crowd that isn't there. A crowd that loves and accepts her.*)

I'LL STAY!

(*As the music builds, she's queen of the magic kingdom. Somewhere in the distance, fireworks. Castles. DORIA waves and waves . . . until . . .*)

CURTAIN

END ACT TWO

[MUSIC #21 *BOWS*]

[MUSIC #22 *EXIT MUSIC*]

CPSIA information can be obtained at www.ICGtesting.com
Printed in the USA
BVOW06s1255200615

405064BV00008B/122/P